FICTION HOUSE PRESS
PRESENTS

MANHUNT

November 1953
Vol. 1, No. 11

This reprint edition is a facsimile of the original pulp magazine. Variations in printing and quality can be attributed to the original magazine which was printed on rough woodpulp paper. No attempt has been made to politically correct any language deemed inappropriate to the modern reader.

New Material

ISBN 978-1-64720-672-7

www.FictionHousePress.com
fictionhousepress@gmail.com

VOL. 1, NO. 11 NOVEMBER, 1953

MANHUNT

CONTENTS

NOVELETTES *Page*

SHORT STORIES

FEATURES

JOHN McCLOUD, *Editor*
HAL WALKER, *Managing Editor*
CHAS. W. ADAMS, *Art Director*
R. E. DECKER, *Business Manager*

MANHUNT Volume 1, Number 11, November, 1953. Single copies 35 cents. Subscriptions, $4.00 for one year in the United States and Possessions; elsewhere $5.00 (in U. S. funds) for one year. Published monthly by Flying Eagle Publications, Inc. (an affiliate of St. John Publishing Company), 545 Fifth Avenue, New York 17, New York. Telephone MU 7-6623.

The Big Touch

A Peter Chambers Novelette

BY HENRY KANE

Anabel was a very high-class stripper, and Anabel was rich. It didn't make sense to Chambers that she'd go into blackmail.

BLACKMAIL is old-fashioned, and there was nothing old-fashioned about Anabel Jolly. Blackmail is dangerous — and although Anabel Jolly was as dangerous a female as ever it had been my pleasure to encounter — the danger involved, piquant and exciting and practically overwhelming, was directed *from* Anabel Jolly *at* all comers (provided such comers were male). And Anabel Jolly wasn't looking for trouble — not blackmail trouble. She didn't need it. Anabel Jolly was loaded. I had put in ten days of intensive spade work before I met her. I knew all about her. She didn't have to break the law to obtain money. She had money. She had plenty of money.

Then why the blackmail pitch?

I intended to ask her. Tonight.

Meanwhile, I sat quietly and watched her take her clothes off. She took her clothes off with grace and spirit, revealing a lush, long-legged, firm-thighed, narrow-waisted, full-bosomed dazzling whiteness, and she strutted proudly, and defiantly. Anabel Jolly had made a good thing of taking off her clothes. It was rumored that she had received as high as $5000 per week for the simple operation, if simple is the word, of removing her clothes under a blue light on a small stage before a select and palpitating public. She had worked all the best clubs in the country, from Hollywood to New York, and right now she was performing her specialty in a club of her own appropriately, if mildly, entitled Club Jolly.

I was part of a packed house, alone at a small round table, and I applauded with the rest of the boobs, and I meant it. Anabel Jolly was a peeler, but she was the best in the business, and the best is always something. Anabel Jolly was an artist. There are others who have the equipment: structure, beauty, grace and rhythm. Anabel Jolly had more. She combined a display of sex with an air of contempt, a warmth of movement with a frigid poise, a voluptuous wriggling body with a cold and arrogant mien: her eyes were slits that viewed the viewers with disdain: it was as though she erected an invisible barrier between herself and her audience: she was naked but untouchable, and out of reach. And the suckers loved it.

She did her last bump, her last grind, stood stock-still with her arms outflung, her body in a crouch, her eyes wide open now, a smile of contempt on her mouth — and the curtain closed about her. The lights came on and the hubbub grew and the waiters stalked the tables. This was the last show and most of the patrons paid their checks and left. I had another drink and waited. I had a date with Anabel Jolly. This was the fifth night running I'd had a date with Anabel Jolly, and I'd enjoyed every one of them, but tonight I was going to put it to her, about the blackmail, and that was a prospect I didn't enjoy. I looked down at my watch. It was a quarter to four in the morning.

The tables around me were wearing their chairs when she finally joined me. She rubbed a cool finger along the back of my neck and said, "Hi, Lover."

Lover grinned upward. "Bar's closed. You can have a sip of mine, if a sip is needful."

"More than one sip is needful, Sweetie. Let's get out of here."

I paid, and we went. It was warm out, a warm night in October, Indian Summer hanging over the town like an omen of doom. I waved to a cab, and we rolled, windows down, toward Harlem, to an after-hours joint called Jackson's. There was dancing in Jackson's, and heavy black drapes over the windows, and Dixieland music, and velvet-throat crooners, and shouters, and name-brand undiluted whiskey, and Southern fried chicken, and Chinese noodles, and barbecued spare-ribs with a secret sauce.

We sat opposite one another under pink indirect lights in an intimate booth and I watched her tear at spare-ribs unabashedly. Her mouth was red and wet and shiny from the grease of the ribs. Her eyes were green and wide, her nose small and tilted, and her red hair was parted in the middle and cut short in a cap of tight glistening Grecian curls. Her dress matched her eyes, green, with puffed sleeves, and a slit down the middle deeper than a pick-pocket's reach. I watched her and hated the fact that she was grist for the mill, part of work, part of business, part of the chase after the ever-elusive buck.

She set down the rib, wiped her mouth with a napkin, sighed, said, "Somehow, Lover, I hate you."

"Me?"

"You. I've been waiting for you to open up. It's five nights now — and nothing."

"Open up?" I sipped Scotch and water.

"Look. Nobody's name can be Timothy Tiddle. Not even yours. How'd I ever get to know you?"

"We were introduced. Remember? By Phil Webster, a mutual acquaintance. You thought I was cute, and I think you're beautiful. What's the problem?"

"Timothy Tiddle, a Texas oil millionaire. Brother, how corny can you get?"

I smiled around the rim of the glass. "What's corny?"

"You, pal. You're no visiting fireman. I'll say this for you. You spend like a Texas millionaire. You're a real welcome customer in my joint. Even the waiters like you, and my waiters are tough to please. But you're no fireman, pal. You're hip, real hip. Why, there ain't a joint in town, real joint, not the square palaces, that you don't know, and where they don't know you. You're not even on the *make* for me, I can tell. You're just being polite, and gentlemanly, and squire-like. Now why in all hell *are* you squiring me around for, kid? Break down and tell little Anabel."

The music was smooth now and there were couples tooling toward the dance floor. I put down my drink and pointed a finger over my shoulder. "Shall we?" I said. Gallantly.

She smiled with all the teeth. "The way you dance, I'd love it."

The floor was small, the lights dim, the music schmaltzy, and all of Anabel Jolly nestled beside me as we swayed on a dime, her mouth at my ear, and vice versa. She whispered, "What's your name, Lover?"

"Peter Chambers."

"You ready?"

There was a moment of silence, then I said, "Yeah."

"I knew it. All the time."

"Knew what?"

"What your name was. Peter Chambers. I'm glad you told me."

I moved my head back and looked at her. For the first time, her eyes were pleased. She winked once, kissed me on the mouth lightly, and put her cheek back against mine. She whispered, "You're a figure around this town, pal. I played out the reel, waiting for action. You're a cop. A private dick, eye, richard — whatever the hell they call them. What's the promotion, pal? You looking to put a padlock on my joint?"

"No."

"I worked hard, and I worked a long time, to get where I am. I pay plenty ice. If I got to heist the ice, okay with me, you're on the payroll. Happens you're cute too. Happens I like you. You're liable to earn your ice, if you know what I mean." Her body pressed closer. "I'm not too hard to take, am I?"

"No."

"We got a deal?"

"No."

Her body went rigid and she said, "Let's break it up, Lover."

Back at our table, I said, "Anabel —"

"Don't Anabel me. You're looking to play it high and mighty, okay, you're looking to have it catch up with you. I've handled tougher babies than you."

"I've got nothing against your joint."

"Say that again. Slow."

"Nothing against your joint. Period."

"Then what's the play?"

"Lemme ask a few questions first. May I?"

"Shoot, Lover. I'm beginning to like you again."

"You're fixed pretty good for dough, aren't you?"

"The best."

"Like how?"

"Like I own the Club Jolly outright. Like I've got a hundred and fifty gees banked, in cash. Like I got a load of government bonds. Like I own a couple of apartment houses in L.A. Like I'm coining dough, every day, hand over fist. It wasn't this good always, but it's good now. I'm Number One in the strip racket. There's always a Number One. There was a Dempsey, a Ruth, a Tilden, a Valentino, a Garbo, a Pavlowa — me, I'm Anabel Jolly. I'm doing a little bit of all right."

"Then what's with blackmail?"

The lids of the green eyes came down like purple shades. One corner of the mouth fought for a smile, but it lost against the other corner: tight, and strained, and unhappy.

"Roger Aldridge," I said. "Six lousy letters. Two hundred and fifty thousand dollars."

"So that's it," she said.

"That's it."

"You working for him?"

"I'm trying."

The smile came, finally, bitter as though she'd bit into a worm. "A fine romance," she said.

"You and me?"

"I had it figured like that. You and me. That's the way I was born. I either go, or I don't go. With you I could go. I figured we could ring a couple of bells together. G'bye, Lover."

"Roger Aldridge?"

"Go pick another doll to be a detective with. G'bye, Lover."

She stood up fast, tilting the table. I wrestled with it, righted it, and got out of the booth — but I was stopped by a waiter with the check. By the time I paid, she was gone. I came out of the warmth of pink dimness into the sad grey of a sunless morning. A few early-go-to-workers straggled by. I whistled down a cab and I went home.

2.

Three o'clock in the office, I put through a call to Roger Aldridge. It was a fancy number, Plaza with a lot of circles. Everything about Roger Aldridge was fancy: his place of business, his mode of dress, his manner of living, his well-modulated voice — even the fee I was going to charge him, plus expenses. When the well-modulated voice came through, I said, "I've talked with her."

Tightly he said, "Save it."

"For when?"

"When can I see you?"

"Anytime. You're the client."

"Would you care to drop over to my apartment?"

"I'd care. When?"

"I can get away now. If it's all right with you."

"You're still the client."

"You know the address?"

"Yes, sir."

"See you in about a half hour."

"Fine."

I hung up, rustled papers on the desk, clamped my lower lip between my fingers and tried to think about my fee, but my thoughts turned about Anabel Jolly. There was no doubt that Roger Aldridge could be touched up for a big figure. The guy was a buyer for a jewelry house, small and exclusive, but one of the top ten in the country. Yet, after all, he *was* an employee, and two hundred and fifty thousand blackmail bucks was a quarter of a million dollars, and that's not horse hair to fill a mattress. He was in good shape for the touch, what with a society wife of two years standing, a brand new kid, and a snobby job with a plush firm — but a quarter of a million is a quarter of a million and like that you make it rough on yourself, Miss Anabel Jolly. You hit a guy for two bits, you might make it stick. But you hit a guy where it hurts, and he howls. Howling can't do you any good, Miss Anabel Jolly. Plus. Plus you don't need the dough.

That makes it crazy. And when it's crazy you can't figure it — not without many more facts. I didn't have much. I had a bare outline. Only what Aldridge had chosen to tell me. He had been recommended by an uncle of his, Donald Root, an old guy with a lot of loot, whose legs were withered and who lived in a wheel chair. Aldridge had told me about six steaming letters he had written to Jolly when he was hot on the make, about five years ago and before he was married. My job was to reconnoitre, mosey around, and find out what it was all about. If I could get back the letters without any trouble, it was worth fifteen thousand dollars. If not, it was my usual fee, plus expenses. I hadn't stated what my usual fee was, and right now it was growing. My orders had been not to be in touch with him until I had something definite.

I grabbed my hat and headed for Aldridge's place. I was either going to collect a lot of facts and really go to work on it, or I was going to collect my fast-growing fee and kiss it off.

Aldridge lived on lower Fifth Avenue high up in a penthouse apartment. An elevator whisked me up and I shoved a finger at his doorbell. The door was opened by a cute maid (this is a guy who keeps begging for trouble) who said, "Yes?"

"Mr. Aldridge in?"

"Yes. Who may I say?"

"Peter Chambers."

"Yes, please come in." She preceded me to a drawing room. She said, "Please make yourself at home. I will tell Mr. Aldridge you are here."

I said, "How long has he been here?"

"He just came in."

Aldridge's voice filtered through from a nearby room. "Who is it, Marie?"

She smiled at me, said, "I'll tell him," went out, and almost at once Aldridge was in the room and we were shaking hands.

"Prompt," he said. "I haven't even had a chance to wash. Don't blame me, do you, for not wanting to talk on the phone? Place of business, that sort of thing."

"Don't blame you in the least. Nice shack you've got here."

"Eleven rooms and costs a fortune, but if you don't put on the dog in my business, you're dead. Love you to meet my wife, but she and the child are visiting her mother uptown. What do you drink, Mr. Chambers? If I don't have a splash, I'll blow up."

"Scotch and water. One cube."

He opened a cabinet and made drinks. He made mine first and handed it to me. For himself he poured half a tumbler of Scotch, added a spray of seltzer, and drank a lot of it in a hurry. He was tall and slim and about forty with blue-grey hair at the temples and a white mustache with waxed ends. He had blue eyes and a trick of squinting them at you when he talked. He said, "Any luck?"

I said, "Hardly."

He didn't like that. He said, "Sit down." He was a man who was accustomed to giving commands. I didn't sit. I stood. He said, "What do you mean by 'hardly?' "

"Anabel Jolly. A hell of a gorgeous dame."

He smiled. Wryly. He said, "You're telling me."

"Not the blackmail type at all."

"What does that mean?"

"Well, in my business, you can sort of spot them."

Brusquely he said, "Matter of opinion. Let's skip that, Mr. Chambers. Let's stick to the facts."

"You're the client."

"That's a pet phrase of yours, isn't it?"

"Matter of opinion. About Anabel Jolly. She doesn't have to deal in blackmail. She's loaded."

"Facts, please, Mr. Chambers."

"I'd say she's worth three-four hundred thousand bucks, at a minimum figure. That's a matter of opinion too, but put that down as expert opinion, after careful investigation. I'd say a dame like that doesn't figure to resort to blackmail, aside from the fact that she's not the type."

"But the fact remains that she has, Mr. Chambers."

"I know it. And it needs talking. You've given me nothing to work on."

"Am I supposed to?"

"That's up to you. I'll say this, though. Unless you do, I'd rather you paid me my fee, and we close up shop."

He finished his drink. "Fee? How much, Mr. Chambers?"

Now I squinted *my* eyes at *him*. "Fifteen days, fifty dollars a day, that's seven fifty, and I'll go easy on the expenses for you. Say, two fifty. That's a thousand dollars, round figure."

He put his drink down, opened his jacket and reached in for a narrow check book and a fountain pen. A holster hung from his belt and a gun was fixed in it.

I said, "You always wear that?"

"What?"

"The gun."

"Yes. In my business, it's a necessary evil. I frequently carry valuable jewelry on my person."

"I understand."

He wrote a check, ripped it out of the book, and handed it to me. It was for a thousand dollars. He went back to the cabinet and made himself another drink. He said, "You're an independent cuss, aren't you?"

I did a grin for him. "And an expensive one."

"That too. I don't mind the expense. I do mind a clash of temperaments."

"You don't have to be in love with a client to work for him. But you do need co-operation."

"Such as?"

"I might be able to help, if you

loosened up a little. You don't go to a doctor, and then hold out on the symptoms."

He paced, glass in hand, sipped, and sat down. "You have a point there, sir."

"Thanks."

"What would you want to know?"

"Well, it's the old cornball deal of letters. Okay. Here's a dame got some hot letters of yours written five years ago. So what? Your wife, to whom you're married two years — she can't object to letters you wrote when you were single."

"The letters were undated, Mr. Chambers. Somehow you don't date love letters as though they were part of a business correspondence. When I had my interview with Miss Jolly at her club, she informed me that she would state that such letters were written within the past few months."

"Check," I said. "I'm sorry." I was beginning to warm up to Mr. Roger Aldridge. Maybe I was getting accustomed to his careful enunciation.

"Five years ago," he said and smiled. "I wasn't quite as conservative as I am now."

"What was the threat? Was she going to present them to your wife?"

"Better than that. A press agent was going to do a story on her for one of the tabloids. She was going to turn the letters over to him, for added spice. And they were supposed to be written within the past few months. Photostats, that sort of thing. Can you imagine what that could do to me?"

"Yeah," I said. I made myself another drink and sat down near him. "I can't figure it. Here's a dame that doesn't need the loot."

"Everybody needs a quarter of a million dollars."

"Not when it's attached to extortion. If you went to the cops with this, and they worked out a plant — that's a felony, Mr. Aldridge. That dame can sit her sweet behind in the pokey for ten years on a deal like this. That's a crazy risk, when you don't need the loot."

"You sure about her monetary situation?"

"Positive. I put ten days on that angle, before I even met her. Why should a dame risk ten years out of the prime of her life when she absolutely doesn't need the money?"

He squinted at me and his teeth clicked along the edge of his glass. "You've got a point there."

"And why now? She's had those letters for five years. Why now, when she's sitting on top of the world, boss-lady of her own club?"

"You still working for me, Mr. Chambers?"

"If you say so."

"I say so."

"Then I'm still working for you."

Roger Aldridge abandoned his drink and stood up out of the chair. He went to a window, peered out, clasped his hands behind his back and spoke to me without looking at me. "I can't inform you about her need for money. I know nothing about that, pro or con. But I think I can answer your question."

"Which one?"

"The one about — why now."

"You mean there's a special reason why she's waited five years?"

"I don't know if she consciously waited five years. But I do know that now — that this particular moment in my career — is most propitious for this kind of hold-up." He turned and came away from the window. "This is in the strictest confidence, Mr. Chambers."

"Of course."

"You know that I'm employed by Winston Parnell."

"Yes?"

"I earn a good deal of money now. About a hundred thousand dollars a year."

"Yes?"

"I'm going to earn more than that."

"How?"

"Mr. Parnell is getting on in years. He's planning to retire. I am slated to take over the full active management of the firm. As a partner."

"I see."

"The lawyers have already prepared the papers. The date for the new partnership is November 15. Miss Jolly got in touch with me early in October. She gave me until November 1 to make up my mind. I'm wondering if there's any connection."

"Yeah," I said. "Yeah."

"You can imagine what will happen to me if this press-agent scheme of hers goes through. The notoriety would definitely finish the deal. Do you understand now why it was worth fifteen thousand dollars to me to obtain the return of those letters?"

"Yeah," I said. "But does Jolly know about your deal?"

He shrugged expressive shoulders. "Frankly, I can't see how. The only ones who know about it are the principals and the lawyers. Except . . ." His Adam's apple jumped as he gulped.

"Who?"

"My cousin, Jonathan Nolan."

"That guy?" I said.

"He used to be a brilliant lawyer."

"Yeah, but he was disbarred last year, wasn't he?"

"Do you know him?"

"No, but I heard about him. From your uncle."

"I have a good deal of confidence in Jonathan; that is, in his brain power. He's a young man, much younger than I, but, no matter what anyone may say about his morals, no one in the world can deny the fact of his brilliance."

"So?"

"When the contracts were finally prepared, I brought them to him for a last check."

"I get it. Does he know Jolly?"

He shook his head sadly. "He does. In fact, he introduced me to her."

"Think there's any connection?"

"I don't think Jonathan would have anything to do with blackmail. Jonathan would use a rapier rather than a bludgeon. No. Wide open blackmail would be too stupid and too risky. It's my best guess that, inadvertently, he dropped the information to Miss Jolly, and Miss Jolly decided to make hay in the sunshine."

"A quarter of a million. That's hay, all right."

"She's got me where it hurts. I'll tell you that, sir."

"Mind if I see Jonathan?"

He looked frightened. "If you think that's all right. But I don't think you ought to mention —"

"I agree with you. If he's in it, if he's using the bludgeon instead of the rapier — then he's in it. But if he's not, he might be an excellent advocate for the good Miss Jolly. Though for the life of me I can't figure that gal. What's his address?"

"He has an apartment at 10 West 35th Street. And a small office at 150 West 42nd Street."

"And who's your lawyer?"

"Warren Dodge."

"The best. A fine old man. He's your uncle's lawyer too."

"That's right."

"I'm going to talk with him too. Does he know about your trouble with Jolly?"

"Nobody knows anything about that except you."

"I think we ought to take Mr. Dodge into our confidence."

He sat down and scraped a finger at a frown on his forehead. "You're the expert in these affairs, Mr. Chambers."

"Thanks," I said. "And thanks for the interview, and thanks for rehiring me."

He took up his glass and drained it. He said, "I've got to do some tall thinking. Tomorrow, I'm off. Suppose I drop in at your office at about two o'clock."

"Sure."

I left him bent in his chair, staring at the floor and rubbing a finger at the frown on his forehead.

3.

The Flatiron Building is a skinny triangle pointing north on 23rd Street. Warren Dodge's office was on the 7th floor and an elderly lady at an ancient desk was his receptionist.

"Peter Chambers," I said, "for Mr. Dodge."

"Do you have an appointment, Mr. Chambers?"

"No, ma'am," I said.

She smiled and wrinkled her nose at me. "I don't know why I ask that question. It's silly. Please sit down. I'll ask Mr. Dodge if he'll see you." She pushed herself out of her chair, waddled to a door, opened it, and said, "There's a young man outside, Peter Chambers. Will you see him?"

Warren Dodge had a booming voice. "Sure I'll see him. I'd love to see him. Send him right in, Mamie. But you could have used the intercom. That's what I've got it for."

"Inter-com." She sniffed. "Gadgets. People spending money for nothing. Giving themselves importance." She turned to me and smiled again. "Mr. Dodge would *love* to see you. In here, please." She held the door open for me while I passed through, then slammed it behind me.

The office had wooden walls and many windows and green filing cabinets and a cluttered desk and the handsome Mr. Dodge behind the desk. Warren Dodge was at least seventy years of age, but he looked fifty, acted forty, and had the zest of thirty. He was a bulky man with a smooth face, round and pink, and short cut tight grey hair, thick as steel wool and kinky as your aunt with arthritis. He was quick to laugh, his teeth were good, and the one eye that had begun to fail him was encased in a monocle.

"Good to see you, lad," he said. "And how goes it with all the little murderers in our fair city?"

"What a business," I said.

"You picked it."

"It's a living."

"You do pretty well, my lad. What's the occasion for a visit to a lawyer?"

"Roger Aldridge."

"Pompous, but well-meaning. Known him since he's a boy."

"Old man Root recommended him."

"And I recommended you to Mr. Root, a long time ago, while he was still active. What was Roger's trouble that Root knew about?"

"Root didn't know what Roger's trouble was. Roger told him he had need of a private detective, and the old man mentioned me."

Warren Dodge stood up. He said, "I smell gossip. I smell an enjoyable conversation. Let's get out of this would-be business-like atmosphere. Come into the library."

He opened a rear door and we went into a cool large book-lined room. There were easy chairs, and a liquor cabinet, and green blinds at the windows holding back the sun.

"Love this room," I said.

"Most rooms, unlike most women, grow more beautiful with age." He chuckled. "Some day I'm going to fire Mamie out there and get me somebody with curves."

"You do all right."

"Well, I'm a bachelor, aren't I? And it happens that I've retained my appreciation for curves."

"Know Anabel Jolly?"

"No. Should I?"

"But curves."

"Then I should."

"Roger Aldridge knows her."

"That the trouble?"

"That's it."

"You free to tell me about it?"

"Yes."

He chuckled again. "Told you I smelled gossip. Sit down. Let me fix a couple of long ones. You're a Scotch man, aren't you?"

"Yes, sir." I moved into a soft leather chair and stretched my legs.

Warren Dodge said, "One cube, if I remember."

"There's not much you forget, sir."

He brought the drinks, set them up on a corner of a library table, backed into a nearby easy chair, bent, opened the laces of his shoes, kicked them off, sighed, took up his drink, said smilingly, "Make it gory, lad . . . or make it sexy."

I told him the story from the time I'd been retained by Roger Aldridge, and his first comment was: "Sounds fascinating, that Anabel Jolly."

"Is fascinating."

"You reserving that?"

"I am."

"For whom?"

"For me."

His eyes grinned. "Too bad. All right. What's this visit for?"

"Well . . . since we both know some of the parties involved . . . I thought it good sense to talk it over with you. I come for advice, Mr. Dodge, and for counsel."

"What are you really here for, Peter?"

"I'd like the lowdown on Jonathan Nolan."

"That's better." He took the monocle out, breathed on it, wiped it with a handkerchief, set it back. "Jonathan Nolan. I'm inclined to agree with Roger. I don't think he'd tamper with blackmail. He's too shrewd, too careful, and . . . too imaginative."

"What's the story on that guy, Mr. Dodge?"

"Brilliant. Too brilliant. Too wise. Too worldly. Too acquisitive. Wanting to get rich, really rich, too quickly."

"How old a guy?"

"Jonathan? Now? Not more than thirty, all told. Brilliant student, quick early success — then, bang."

"How'd the bang happen?"

"Let's begin from the beginning, eh?"

"It's your story, sir."

"Jonathan Nolan." He sighed and the eye behind the monocle closed in reminiscence. "A wild kid, and headstrong. An orphan, as was Roger. Brought up by the uncle, Donald Root. These two boys are his only legal heirs, his only heirs at law. Two boys reared in the same environment, one crazy-wild, the other quiet and stuffy."

"About Jonathan . . ." I said.

"He got out of law school at the age of twenty-two. That was about the time Donald Root's wife died. At that time, Mr. Root gave up his estate in Scarsdale, and took his apartment in town. You know where he lives, an old-fashioned narrow little house on Park Avenue. A splendid old house, five stories high, but nothing pretentious, no doorman, self-service elevator — quiet and dignified. And there Mr. Root lives to this day, an invalid now, attended only by Emerson Beach, valet, cook, and chauffeur."

"About Jonathan . . ." I said.

"He gave each of them a present, the younger Jonathan, and the older Roger . . . fifty thousand dollars each . . . and they were on their own, living apart, no longer part of the household."

"Now, about Jonathan . . ."

"As you know, his will mentioned only them . . . Jonathan and Roger . . . to share alike of his estate upon his decease." He held up a hand, said, "Yes, yes . . . about Jonathan. He practiced law, and he practiced it in a hurry . . . but he was a professional boxer, for a while, on the side."

I felt my eyebrows fly up. "A professional boxer?"

"He had been intercollegiate heavyweight champ. Friends prevailed on him to enter the professional domain. He did, felt he wasn't good enough, and went back to practicing law in a hurry."

"What do you mean . . . practicing law in a hurry?"

"Obtaining negligence cases through unethical means, handling unsavory cases that other lawyers wouldn't handle . . . making a lot of money, and always spending a bit more than he made . . . and gathering a bad reputation along the way. Donald Root called him in and warned him. As did the bar association, after several complaints. Then he became a boxing manager."

"A *boxing* manager?"

"Behind-the-scenes boxing manager, but it heralded an era of more fixed fights than the boxing business has ever known. Again he made a good deal of money, and again he spent a good deal of money . . . but it finally caught up with him. His sheer brilliance, his planning, his cunning . . . prevented his going to jail. Six others were found guilty, and sentenced . . . but there was insufficient evidence for his conviction, and he was acquitted."

"Any money left?"

"Very little. But the bar association didn't need the quality of evidence required by a criminal court — proof of guilt beyond a reasonable doubt. And certain evidence that, in our jurisprudence, was inadmissible in a court of law, *was* admissible to the bar association sitting in committee. Jonathan Nolan was disbarred."

"When?"

"One year ago. And at that time, as Mr. Root once informed you, he changed his will. Jonathan was cut off. One half of Root's estate goes to Roger Aldridge, the remainder to charity. A simple half-page will replaced the old one."

"And how's Jonathan fixed for money at present?"

"Not too well, from what I hear."

"What's he doing now?"

"He's a bookmaker."

"A *what?*"

"A bookmaker."

I finished my drink and I stood up. "Good bye, Mr. Dodge."

"Where to now, lad?"

"Jonathan Nolan."

"Careful does it."

"Careful? Why?"

"He hits first and he asks questions later. And he's thoroughly capable. Wild and headstrong, and very clever. He hasn't changed."

"Thanks for the information." I winked at him and waved my hand. "And thanks for the advice. Take care."

"You too."

4.

The black wall-bulletin in the lobby of 150 West 42nd Street said J. NOLAN . . . 1401 . . . in white celluloid replaceable letters. The elevators were in the rear and I went there and waited amongst a small knot of prospective passengers. The elevator arrived with a rattle like dungeon chains and we entered and each of us sounded off with the number of his floor. I got out at 14 and walked a long narrow corridor to 1401. It was a door with a glaze-glass window with no printing on it except the number: 1401. Adjacent was another door, of metal, stating in red letters: STAIRWAY. I tried that door first. It opened on a stairway landing, cool, dim and deserted. I closed that door and tried 1401. It gave on one push.

I was in a square room with a stone floor and no furniture except a narrow desk with a swivel chair behind it and a wooden armchair in front of it. There was a covey of five telephones on the desk, an ashtray, and a long pad of yellow paper with a pencil on it. That was it.

A tall young man was pacing the floor when I entered. He was broad-shouldered and lithe with black hair parted on the side, black eyes, a firm jaw, a jutting chin, and a pale face. He wore an oxford grey suit, a white button-down shirt, and a yellow and black striped tie. The suit had a vest. There was a chain going from pocket to pocket of the vest, and a gold boxing glove hung from the middle of the chain. He threw me a quick look, lifted a smooth black eyebrow, went to the swivel chair, slid down, injected a thin cigar in a corner of his mouth and cocked it like a field gun.

I said, "Jonathan Nolan?"

He said, "That's right." He angled the chair, lifted his legs, banged his heels on the desk top and left them there.

My cue was to work out a connection, if any, between Jonathan Nolan and Anabel Jolly, and my tactic was quick-job chatter and see what happens. I said, "Anabel sent me."

Color came up in Jonathan Nolan's face and stayed there like a stuck elevator. His heels scraped off the desk. He leaned forward in the swivel chair and said, "Come again?"

"Anabel Jolly."

"Who the hell is Anabel Jolly?"

"A twist, with a twist. Who's cutting me in. I'm supposed to come and see you. You and me, we're supposed to talk about it."

The elevator came unstuck. Color receded from his face. "Talk about what?"

"Quiet money. There's people call it blackmail. There's all kinds of amateurs. I'm a professional. Quiet money is my business. Ask Anabel. You move up to the kind of money that counts, you need the professional touch. Anabel says I'm to see you. So I'm seeing you."

"What's your name?"

"Bellows. Gus Bellows."

The black eyes stayed on mine, then dropped. The right hand went to the jacket pocket and for a moment I thought I was going to have gun trouble. But the hand came up with a packet of matches, and I relaxed. He lit the point of the cigar and flung the packet onto the desk. He puffed, hard, until there was a good deal of smoke between us and the point of the cigar flattened to a red blaze. Then he flung it, burning end forward, right at my face, and as I jumped to duck, he came after it, one spring over the desk. A thick right jolted me to the floor. Two hands grabbed the hair of my head, raised it and smashed the back of it against the stone floor. His face bulged out in front of me, whirled . . . then blackness.

5.

One leg moved first, then the other leg, then I heard a groan. I lay flat on my back and listened. I heard another groan, and then another, before I realized it was I who was groaning, so I stopped. My legs moved again and I tried to get up but I couldn't make it. I rolled over, prone. There was a numbness in back of my head. I pulled my knees up under me and pushed against the cold floor with my knees and my hands and my forehead and I began to come up, the middle of me first, but then I got tired and I dropped. I rested on my face, a throbbing replacing the numbness in back of my head. Then I did it again, the same way, knees and hands and forehead pushing, back end coming up first. Then I got my forehead off the floor, got a foot under me, grabbed at a ledge with my hand, and pulled myself up. I heard the slap of something dropping, but I didn't care. I was facing a wall, and I leaned on it, panting. Then I began to breathe more deeply. I was able to shake my head against oncoming nausea. I fought it down, shaking my head all the time like a dog out of water. The area stopped swaying and straightened out.

I was on the landing on the other side of the door marked STAIRWAY. The ledge that my hand was holding was the bannister. I let go, touched the back of my head, and looked at my hand. It was dry. I looked down to see what had dropped. There were two things. There was my wallet and there were my credentials as an investigator. The good Mr. Nolan must have thrown those into my lap, like you throw a sneer at a wise guy, when the wise guy turns out to be stupid. I'd turned out to be just that. I'd gotten action from Mr. Nolan before I had expected action. Faintly,

I promised myself that the action between Mr. Nolan and myself had only begun.

Double vision hit me again. I didn't stoop for my stuff and the wallet. Instead, I slid down to the top step, sat, stuck my head deep down between my knees, and drew big sops of breath. I sat like that for ten minutes and I began to feel better. I reached for the wallet, shoved the stuff into it, put the wallet into a pocket, and pulled myself up to standing. I opened the door and I was out in the corridor. I fell against 1401, turned the knob and pushed, but it was locked. I made it to the elevator, fluttering like a loose pair of drawers hung out in a stiff breeze.

The elevator boy's face lengthened. "What happened, bub?"

"Slipped in the hall. Banged my head."

"We'll go down express. Talk to the starter."

Downstairs, the starter said, "Was there anything wrong up there, anything slippery? I'll send up the boy for a look. Anything wrong, you put in a claim. We run this building de luxe. I'll make a report on it right away."

"No. Nothing wrong. No report. Just got my two left feet mixed up. My own fault. If you'd help me to a cab, I'd appreciate it."

"Sure, Jack."

I gave the cabbie my doctor's address, and fifteen minutes later, I was sprawled under an X-ray machine. I was feeling much better. He had given me a shot in the arm, a pill to swallow, and water to drink that had tasted as lousy as all water tastes from a paper container. Then he had touched my head, murmured about "Hematoma," and led me to the X-ray machine. I rested on a cot while the plates were being developed. Then the doctor came to me, smilingly.

"Nothing harder than a hard head," he said. "You had me worried, but there's no fracture. But I want you off your feet for a couple of hours. Will you do that for me?"

"Not here. I'm allergic to cots since the Army."

"No. I'll take you upstairs, put you up in a nice comfy bedroom, give you a nice comfy pill, and you'll sleep for a nice comfy couple of hours."

I looked at my watch. It was a nice comfy six o'clock.

"Okay," I said.

Upstairs, with my clothes off, in bed with a pillow under my head, I staved off the pill with upraised hand. "Can I make a couple of phone calls first?"

"Sure."

"Phone book?"

He brought me a phone book and took his pill away with him. I looked up Jonathan Nolan on West 35th Street. I dialed the number. There was no answer. Then I called Warren Dodge at home. He answered quickly. I said, "Mr. Dodge, one question."

"Who is this?"
"Peter Chambers."
"What's your question, son?"
"Jonathan Nolan. He married?"
'Bachelor."
"Lives on West 35th Street?"
"Last I heard."
"Thanks, Mr. Dodge."
"That all?"
"That's all."
"Real mysterious."
"Got to go to sleep now. Thanks, Mr. Dodge."
"Sleep? I beg your pardon? What? What was that?"
"Bye, now. Thanks."
I hung up. I called Nolan's number again. I let it ring a long time. There was no answer. Then I checked the phone book for M. Russell, Locks and Keys, 850 Sixth Avenue. I called the number and it was answered on one ring. I said, "Mel?"
"Just a minute."
Another voice came on. "Hello?"
"Mel?"
"Yeah."
"Peter."
"Peter who?"
"Pete Chambers."
The voice brightened. "Hi, shamus."
"You free right now?"
"Always free for you, shamus. You're my boy."
"I need a job, quick and clean. But you've got to go out on it right away. Name's Jonathan Nolan. Address 10 West 35th Street. I want a key to get in. You're gonna have to slip up there fast for an impression job. He's not home now, so now is fine. I just called him. You call, just for a double check, before you start working your magic. He's in the phone book. Got it, pal?"
"Got it, pal."
"Go to it."
"When do you want delivery?"
"Tonight. Will your wife let you out tonight?"
I could feel his grin. "Not if she knows it's you. I'll say it's poker."
"Fine. I'll meet you at 11 o'clock. Club Jolly. Okay?"
"You twisted my arm."
"Okay. Go to work." I hung up. I called: "Doc." He came into the room. I said, "All right, put me to sleep. But I've got to be up at ten-thirty."
"Depend on me. Now stick your tongue out."
He put a pill on it, and I gulped water.

6.

Club Jolly was jumping. The band was beating it up like the bennies were being overworked. Cigarette smoke put a ceiling under the ceiling. The customers were buzzing, the waiters were scampering for drinks, the tiny dance floor was getting a workout (as were the dancers), and an aura of expectation quivered over the joint: it was 11 o'clock. Anabel Jolly went on at 11:30, then it was each hour on the half-hour, four times after that.

I waited at a wall table. Then the maître d' brought Mel Russell down to me, Mel in a blue serge suit and a wide grin. He sat down beside me and ordered a drink. I said, "How'd it go?"

"Wrap up. It's apartment 2E. Happy hunting." He produced a key and handed it to me.

"That all?" I said.

"One key. Period."

"How much?"

"Twenty-five bucks. For you. And I split the tab here."

"Never mind that. The tab here's on me. Enjoy." I paid him, and put the key in my pocket.

"Anabel Jolly," he said. "Wow."

"Have you seen her?"

"Nope. But I heard."

The music ceased. The dancers straggled back to their tables. The curtains closed, the dim lights grew dimmer, there was a roll on the drums, and a blue spot played on the shimmering curtains. Then the curtains parted, the music grew torchy and Anabel Jolly's warm-up appeared: a slender girl with a bosom as flat as old beer and a throaty voice. She sang six sick love songs, and went away. The curtains closed again, the dimness turned black, and then the curtains parted to Anabel Jolly.

When it was over, Mel Russell wiped sweat from his brow and said, "Murder."

"Would you like to meet her?"

"Brother, would I?"

I sent the waiter back with a message, and the waiter came back with a message for me. "Miss Jolly," he said, "says no."

Mel said, "You're slipping."

"Must be," I said. "You want to sit around and see it over?"

"How long?"

"An hour."

"Do you?"

"I'm going. I've got a headache. In back of my head."

"You're really slipping, Pete. Time was you couldn't be pried out of a joint like this till closing."

"Yeah," I said. "You want a substitute for me?"

"Like what?"

"Like a female."

"Sure," he said. "As long as I'm playing poker, I may as well play poker."

I paid the check, tipped the waiter, shook hands with Mel, and on the way out I tipped the maître d', whispered to him and pointed at Mel.

"Leave it to me," said the maître d'.

Outside, I used a phone booth in an all-night drug store. I called Jonathan Nolan. There was no answer. I rubbed at a sharp pain in back of my head, had an argument with myself, and I lost. I decided to go home and go to bed.

7.

At 2 o'clock Roger Aldridge presented himself at my office. There was a criss-cross of bags beneath his eyes and he looked tired. "I believe," he said, "my initial error was bringing those contracts to Jonathan. The more I think about it, the more I believe that that precipitated this series of events. But it's easy to be wise — after the fact."

"Second guessers never win."

"Be that as it may, I am very near a decision."

"You're the client."

"I'm going to pay, Mr. Chambers. What do you say to that?"

"I say you're nuts."

"Why?"

"Because blackmail never ends."

"But I'd get back those letters. That's all she has — that's irrefutable."

"She can make photostats. It can go on and on."

"No," he said. "I'd pay, and effect the return of six letters." Then, coldly, he added: "If she monkeyed with me after that — I'd kill her."

"Simple as that?"

"Yes. Essentially I'm a meek man, and I'm willing to compromise —"

"Two hundred and fifty thousand dollars. That's a lot of compromise."

"But even the meekest of us, jockeyed into a corner, and then pushed . . . we'll jump. I'll make a business deal with her, but, if after that she tries any funny stuff — I'll kill her. And I'll tell her that."

I lit a cigarette. I said, "How's it figure?"

"A partnership in Winston Parnell would mean approximately three hundred thousand dollars a year to me. The kind of notoriety she plans would wreck it. I consider it good business, in these circumstances, to pay the equivalent of one year's earnings, to protect such earnings for the rest of my working life. Do you see my point, sir?"

"Yes, I suppose I do. Have you got that kind of dough? To spare?"

"Frankly, I don't. I earn a good deal of money, but what with taxes and my necessary mode of living — my savings are meagre."

"Then how are you going to pay it?"

"I've decided to discuss it with my uncle. You know about his will."

"Yes."

"It's common knoweldge . . . well, family knowledge . . . that he's worth about a half million dollars in cash. It is also no secret that half of that goes to me upon his death, the other half to charity. I propose to ask him to lend me that half right now . . . to be returned by me in three yearly installments."

"You going to tell him what it's about?"

"I'm going to tell him the entire story. Which brings me to another point. I should like a favor from you."

"Me? A pleasure."

"My uncle has a great deal of confidence in you. I have an appointment with him for three o'clock. I should like you to come there, say . . . five . . . five o'clock. You'll corroborate my facts. And today's the best day to talk with him."

"Why today?"

"It's Emerson Beach's day off."

"Emerson Beach?"

"Uncle's valet."

"Oh, yes."

"Well, he leaves in the morning and doesn't return until five o'clock. That gives me two hours alone with my uncle, just the two of us, all alone. Then, you'll come, and I've also asked Warren Dodge to drop by. Like that, my uncle will know the whole story, and he'll be able to have a rounded view, the opinion of each of us. Will you come, Mr. Chambers?"

"Sure."

"Thank you. Thank you very much."

He rose and we shook hands and he went away. I killed my cigarette and went to the window. I saw him come out of the building and hail a cab. Another cab, parked at the curb, shot out after his. I had a hunch that Roger Aldridge had grown a tail.

8.

Donald Root lived on Park Avenue near Sixty-ninth Street. It was a white edifice, a midget between giants, a narrow building of five stories between two skyscrapers, a mark of individuality to the stubborn owner who refused to dispose of his property (at fabulous offers) at the constant behest of the builders for the cliff-dwellers.

It had none of the Park Avenue trappings. There was no doorman, no inside man, no starched dickeys, no canopy, no downstairs switchboard. You opened a brass-bound glass-brick door to a small, immaculate lobby. There was a marble floor, a mahogany side-table, a lamp, a mirror, a self-service elevator, and a cool silence. Each floor had one apartment of five rooms, and each tenant was a carefully selected individual of means and culture.

It was exactly five o'clock when the elevator door slid open for me. I pushed the button for 4, rose silently, and emerged to a carpeted foyer. There was one door, the door to Donald Root's apartment, and the door was ajar. I pushed a button which produced a two-tone tinkle, but produced nothing else. I repeated the two-tone tinkle, waited, then shoved in. I went through a small vestibule into a vast drawing room. Donald Root was in his wheel chair behind his desk. There was a small hole in his forehead and his lifeless chin drooped on his chest.

Roger Aldridge was sprawled face down on the thick red carpet. There was a gun in his hand.

I moved fast. The gun was Roger's gun: his holster was empty. He had a blue welt on his forehead over his right eye. His position was such that he seemed to have been going away: his head was toward the door. The point of one shoe was wedged in a slit of the red carpet where the carpet appeared to be torn. I looked up. There was a bullet hole in the ceiling.

The bullet hole in the ceiling convinced me. I stooped, tore out a tuft of the red carpet, pocketed it, and went to Donald Root. I put my ear against his heart to listen for a beat because that is the thing to do, but there was no question. Donald Root was dead. And the expression on his face had died with him: fear and surprise. I lifted his chin and looked at it: fear and surprise. Then I let the chin go and looked at the paper in front of him on the desk. It was his will, and he had just changed it. His fountain pen was still in his rigid hand.

I read the will quickly. It was entirely in the handwriting of Donald Root. It was the will he had told me about, the one Warren Dodge had mentioned, a half page deal, leaving half his estate to Roger Aldridge and the other half to charity. There was no residual clause. It was signed, and attested by two witnesses. But he had added to it. Beneath his signature, between the attestation clause and the signatures of the witnesses, he had added, in his own handwriting:

> "I hereby bequeath an additional two hundred and fifty thousand dollars to my nephew, Roger Aldridge."

That was all. There was nothing else.

I bent over, examining the carpet at the point in which Roger's shoe was caught, and that was my position when I thought I heard the elevator door open and close. I was slapping at Roger's face, slapping him back to consciousness, when I saw the two feet standing near me. I looked up to the white-pale face of Emerson Beach.

"What . . . ?" he gasped. "What's happened?"

"This is the way I found them. Five minutes ago."

His fingers trembled in the direction of Donald Root. "Is he . . . ? Is he . . . ?"

"He's dead. You'd better call the police. Right now."

9.

One hour later, Roger Aldridge had been booked for murder, and I was frantically trying to find Warren Dodge. I showed up at the Flatiron Building just as Mamie was closing up shop.

"You've been calling and calling," she said.

"Have you heard from him?"

"No, I haven't. But that's not unusual. He left rather late."

"When?"

"He left here at four-thirty."

"Did he say where he was going?"

"To Donald Root's."

"Well, he never showed up there."

"That's not unusual either. Mr. Dodge frequently gets detoured."

Just then the phone rang. Mamie picked it up, said hello, listened. Her mouth opened and she turned greener than a yokel with his last drink on his first binge. She hung up. She said, "He's in a hospital."

"Where?"

"The Flower."

We didn't say a word to each other as the cab fought the going-home traffic. At the hospital, I paid and we ran up the steps. We inquired at the office, and the elevator took us to the 11th floor. A young doctor said, "You first," to Mamie.

I said, "May I see him too?"

"Wait here. We'll be out in a few moments."

I paced the corridor, trying to forget the hospital smells, and then they were out of his room, and coming toward me, and Mamie was wiping her eyes with a handkerchief.

"I told him you were here," she said. "He wants to see you. He's ordered me to go home."

"Nothing you can do here," the young doctor said. "He's to stay at least over-night, perhaps more."

Mamie squeezed my arm, then turned away and proceeded toward the elevators. To the young doctor I said, "What happened?"

"Emergency when we picked him up. Severe concussion, and eleven stitches in his head. He shouldn't see visitors, but he insists on you. Don't stay more than five minutes."

The smell of ether was strong in the room. The bed was cranked up to a half sitting position. Warren Dodge had his eyes closed and his face was paper-white. Bandages and adhesive tape made a tight skull cap on his head. He opened his eyes, saw me, tried for a smile, and missed. He said, "Hi, Peter."

"Hi."

His eyes slid to the doctor. "I want to talk to my friend. Alone, if you please."

"No more than five minutes."

I nodded and the doctor went out.

"What happened?" I said.

Weakly he said, "I was slugged."

"Where?"

"The downstairs lobby at Donald Root's."

"Who slugged you?"

"I told the police I didn't know. I was slugged from behind."

"Robbery?"

"No."

His eyes closed again and there was silence except for the rattle in his throat from his breathing. Then his eyes opened.

I said, "Slugged. But why? What motive?"

He winked. He looked different without his monocle, tired, and old, and somewhat pathetic. "I told the police I didn't know who, but I do."

"Then why didn't you tell them?"

"Because it would have been my word against his. And that isn't proof. And he doesn't think I know. Which gives me a weapon."He shook his head slowly. "I don't understand it."

"What happened, Mr. Dodge? We've only got five minutes."

"I want you to work on it. Bill me if necessary."

"I'll work on it. But give me the story."

He drew a deep breath, and exhaled in an ether-smelling blast. "I was due at Mr. Root's. I was a little early. I entered the lobby and pushed the button for the elevator. The indicator showed it was at 4. I turned my back on it as it was coming down. I was wiping my monocle, when the blow came. The elevator had opened and a passenger had stepped out. As the blow came, I glanced upward, at the mirror, and I saw him. Then it struck. It was the back end of a pistol. For the life of me, I can't understand it. That's your job, Peter. If I ever get out of here, I want to know why he struck me. He doesn't know I saw him."

"Who?"

"Jonathan Nolan."

10.

Detective-Lieutenant Parker tilted his chair back and blew cigar smoke. Parker, out of homicide, was a straight cop with no curves. He set the chair back on its four legs, leaned his elbows on his desk, and said: "Who's the dame, Pete?"

"Dame?" I said.

"Who was holding Aldridge up for blackmail?"

"Parker," I said. "If he won't tell you, I won't tell you. I play ball, but you don't expect me to stool on a client. You don't, do you?"

"No. I don't." He sat back and smoked his cigar. His office was small and neat. "Very gallant, Roger Aldridge. Part of his story is good, part of it stinks out loud."

"Matter of opinion. What's his story?"

"Dame was holding him up for a quarter of a million, and he'd decided to pay it. Went to the uncle for a big loan. Was talking with the uncle, all alone, when the bell tinkled. Went to answer the door, but there seemed to be nobody there. Suddenly, he got hit a blow on the forehead. The lights went out for him. When he came to, the old man was dead, the will was changed, and the gun was in his hand. That's *his* story."

"What's your story?"

"Mine has a lot of evidence to back it up, which is why Roger's in the can. We accept the first part of it. He went to the old man for dough. From there we see it different. We say he got ideas. We say he used his gun as a threat for the old man to change his will. Under duress, the old man did just that. Then we say he knocked him off. Ballistics prove the bullet was from that gun. Serial number shows it was his gun. Paraffin shows he fired it. Then, we say, he tried to beat it, got his foot tangled in the carpet in his hurry to get out. It tore, and he flopped, hit his head, passed out, and that's how you found him."

"What about the bullet in the ceiling?"

"Missed, the first try."

"Pretty wide miss."

"Could happen, when you're excited."

"Did you examine that torn carpet?"

"We examine everything."

"Could have been cut, rather than torn."

"Could have been, but we say it was torn. He'd have to prove different."

"Would a guy use his own gun to commit murder?"

"He had it on him. The idea was an impulse. He was on his way to get rid of it."

"Would he have invited me to come there?"

"Same answer. The idea shaped up as impulse. He'd have been out of there, if he hadn't tripped himself up, before either you or the butler would have shown up. Why do you look at me cockeyed like that? You got a better story?"

"I hope to have."

"When?"

"Soon as I have, I'll let you know. By the way, you keeping Aldridge here over night?"

"Yep."

"Will I be able to see him?"

"Why not?"

"Thanks, pal. And don't go overboard."

"Why?"

"Because *I've* got a story coming up. Soon. Very soon, I hope."

II.

Anabel Jolly lived in a penthouse on Central Park South. I had taken her home, several times, but only to the door: I had never been in the apartment. It was on the 16th floor, with an orange lacquered door, and a sliding peep-hole with a mirrored front. She figured to be in. Anabel Jolly went to sleep in the morning so evening was early afternoon for her. But she had run out on me at Jackson's and she had refused to see me at the Jolly — I wasn't taking any chances.

The boy took me up to the 16th floor. We were alone in the elevator. I said, "Miss Jolly in?"

"I think so. I ain't taken her out."

"Will you ring her bell, please?"

"Bell? What for?"

"Deliver a message."

He put a stay against the elevator door and left it open. In the aisle near her door he said: "What's the message, mister?"

"Me."

"What?"

"I'm the message."

His eyebrows moved down. "I don't get it."

I took a twenty dollar bill out of my wallet, waved it once and slowly, folded it and handed it to him. "You ring the bell, she flips the peep-hole, she sees it's you, you say you got a message, and I take over from there. Okay?"

Now his eyebrows were up, and his grin was a half-grin, tentative, but costly. A second twenty convinced him. He improved on my directions. He rang the bell, and we waited. Then the peep-hole moved, an eye was applied, and Anabel's voice said, "What is it, Oscar?"

"Got a package for you, ma'am."

The door opened and I wedged a foot in. Then I shoved hard on the door, knocked her back, entered, and shut the door behind me. And locked it. She came toward me, her green eyes hot with fury.

"Easy does it," I said. "Remember me? We were going to ring bells together. Timothy Tiddle."

"Bells," she said. "Hell."

"Easy, baby."

"What the hell do you think you're trying to pull here?"

Think? Who could think? Anabel Jolly was wearing a negligee and high-heeled house shoes. The house-shoes were pink and open at the toes. The negligee was diaphanous. Diaphanous. If diaphanous is gauzy pink transparence, if diaphanous is a beautifully carved white marble moving statue veiled in the sheerest pink, if diaphanous improves the unimprovable, enhances the unenhanceable, sets the heart to hammering and beats the blood up to the brain — then diaphanous is the word.

She kept coming at me, the wild green fury in her eyes, and her hands out like claws. I grabbed her. Mostly in self-defense. Mostly. But not all. I grabbed her by the wrists, and forced her hands behind her and into the small of her back, and bent her forward and toward me until her body was tight against mine, and then I captured her mouth with my mouth, and she struggled hard as I kissed her, and then she didn't struggle quite so hard, and then she didn't struggle at all.

I released her soft wet lips and moved my mouth to her ear. I said. "I'm not breaking in here to play potsy. A guy's been murdered, and your name's liable to crop up at any moment. That's why I'm here."

Then I let her go.

She remained where she was, her hands at her sides, the shine of faint tears in her eyes, the soft curves of her body molded to mine. Then her hands moved up and touched my cheeks. Then, lightly, she kissed a corner of my mouth. Then she smiled and she said, "Come in, punk."

There was a breeze in the living room from the terrace. There were rose lights and three large divans with many silk pillows, and two contiguous walls were entirely of amber-colored blocks of mirror. There was a fireplace and andirons and easy chairs and a bar and gay stools and an original *Cobelle* on one wall. She dropped into an easy chair and crossed her long legs and now the white marble of one thigh was exposed, gleaming in the rose light of the room. She said, "What's it all about, Lover?"

"Roger Aldridge."

Her expression tightened. "You still butting into that?"

"It's beyond that now."

"Beyond what?"

"My butting in."

"I don't understand."

"Do you know Donald Root?"

"No."

"Ever hear of him?"

"No."

I brought her a cigarette, lit it for her, lit one for myself. She said, "Sit here. Near me."

I sat where the view was better. Across from her.

I told her about Donald Root. I told her about Roger Aldridge. I told her about Jonathan Nolan. I told her about Warren Dodge. I filled her in from the time I was retained to right now. If she was hustling for blackmail, then my hunch was wrong, and I'd tipped my mitt — and let her take advantage of me. I said exactly that, and I was through. I sat back and let her take it from there.

She didn't move. Her legs were uncrossed now, her knees apart, the pink negligee ruffled in little mounds at her heels. Her pinky was in her mouth and she was biting at the fingernail and a tiny pucker between her eyes was a frown.

She said, "Thanks for the vote of confidence."

"Skip it."

She said, "You're nice."

"Skip that too."

She said, "You think Roger killed his uncle?"

"No."

She said, "You're sweet."

"Honey, we haven't got time for that kind of stuff now."

She stood up, suddenly, wrapped the negligee around her, turned, and slowly walked away, swayingly. My breath caught in my throat. It was something to see. Then she was out of the room and I jumped for the bar and snatched a quick drink for resuscitation. I was in the process of snatching another drink for further resuscitation when she returned. She placed a folded packet in my hand and she said, "You just earned yourself fifteen thousand dollars. Thanks again for the vote of confidence."

I didn't unfold the packet.

She said, "Six letters. From Roger Aldridge to Anabel Jolly. Original letters. There ain't no copies, no photostats, no nothing."

I slipped the packet into a pocket. I said, "What's the story, honey?"

She moved to a divan, threw herself on it, lay there prone, every curve of her accentuated, and cupped her chin in her hands. I knocked down the second drink fast.

She said, "I don't know *what* the story is. But I can tell you my end."

"Let's have it, huh?"

Her hands moved out from under her chin. She cocked a finger, beckoned with it, then patted the divan beside her. "Come here, Lover."

I went. Because it was business.

I sat rigid beside her, and listened.

She turned on her side as she talked. "Roger wrote these things a long time ago. I save that kind of stuff. For laughs. That's all the guy ever was to me — a couple of laughs. I pick my men. And they're few and far between. It's got to be a guy that gives me a tingle, a jingle, a guy I can ring bells with."

"So?"

"Who can ring bells with Roger Aldridge?"

"So?"

"So, after a while, he cooled off, and that was that. Now we come to Jonathan Nolan."

"Could you ring bells with him?"

"I could ring bells with you, Lover."

"We were up to Nolan."

"Nolan was my lawyer. A flip guy, and a wise guy, but a shrewdie. He did me a favor once, and I don't forget a favor."

"What kind of favor?"

"Two years ago, I was contemplating opening the Club Jolly. I had to buy the building. I had a lot of jack at the time, but I didn't have enough. I was short twenty-five thousand bucks. Nolan was always quick with a dollar — to earn it, to spend it, to lend it. He was handling the deal. When this emergency popped up — these things happen in a deal — he advanced the dough. Of course, he took back a mortage, and there was interest plus a bonus — but the guy was there with the buck when I needed it, and I don't forget."

"Did he get his money back?"

"Within two months. Then later on, he got into trouble, he got disbarred, he went broke, and he sort of passed out of my sphere of things."

"Did he know about Roger's letters?"

"Yeah. We had a giggle about them a few times."

"Let's bring it up to date now, eh?"

"Sure. About three weeks ago, Nolan dropped into the club. He was loaded. He's a trouble guy, a muscle guy. He got into an argument with a customer, and he belted him. The guy went back on him, and Nolan slugged him with a bottle. That's bad for business, bad for my license. The guy was hustled out and patched up. Nolan wound up in my dressing room, where I had him sleep it off."

"Muscle guy," I said. "Sister, that bird is begging for it."

"Every hard guy, sooner or later, catches up with a harder one. It hasn't happened to Nolan yet."

"Hasn't it?" I said.

"Anyway, after a snooze and about a gallon of coffee, he straightened out, and he began to beef to me about how he was broke, and how tough things were. Then he had a bright idea. I could help."

"How?"

"That blackmail thing — but without blackmail."

"Now isn't that a cute one. How's it work?"

"He asked me to co-operate. He said I couldn't get into trouble, because it wouldn't really be blackmail."

"What would it be — really?"

"A gag that figured to produce some dough — for him."

"How?"

"Like this. I was to get in touch with Roger and pretend I was going to hold him up — just as I did. But I wasn't going through with it. My job was to speak my piece, and let it lay there, period. Then, according to Nolan, Roger would come to him, and Nolan would be the hero — for a price. Like that, it wouldn't cost me anything, I'd be returning a favor to a guy who helped me out once — and Nolan would be able to pick up some dough he needed badly."

"Only instead of going to Nolan, Roger came to me."

"So it seems."

"You think he was giving you straight goods?"

"Right now, I don't know. That guy's a deep one. I thought it was straight goods at the time he sprung it. What do you think?"

"I don't know either. But I'm gonna know. Thanks, Anabel. I'm getting out of here."

Her hand came up to my neck and a fingernail scraped gently at my hair. Her eyes were lazy as she tilted her head upward. Softly she said, "What's your hurry, Lover?"

It was rough — but I thought of Aldridge in the can, Root in the morgue, and Dodge in the hospital. It was rough — but it would have to keep. I bent down, moved her head away, and kissed the back of her neck. "It'll have to keep," I said, and I stood up.

She looked at me. She didn't move, lying stretched on the divan, topside down, long and curved and lovely and graceful. Then one leg came up, bent at the knee, long and tapered, waving slowly in the air, the arch of the foot high, the toes pointed. Her lips rounded into the shape of a kiss, and one eye closed slowly.

"It'll keep."

I was at the door when she called: "Will you be in touch?"

"Where'll you be?"

"Right here."

"I'll be in touch."

"I'll be waiting."

12.

In the pokey, I talked with Roger Aldridge while Parker hovered nearby. Parker was a gentleman. He stayed out of earshot. I gave Aldridge the letters and he gave me back an incredulous stare. He read them, re-read them, said, "You're a wizard."

"There are no copies," I said. "What you've got — is all there is."

Aldridge looked toward Parker. "Lieutenant," he called.

Parker joined us. "What?"

"May I have my checkbook, Lieutenant? And a pen?"

Parker looked from him to me, said, "Sure," called to a uniformed man, said, "Mr. Aldridge needs his checkbook. And a pen. It's okay." Then Parker went away from us again.

Aldridge said, "How'd you get them?"

I brought him up to date.

He said, "You'll destroy them, Mr. Chambers. We can't do it here. Burn them. I know I can depend on you."

"They're as good as burnt right now."

He was silent for a few moments. Then he said, "What do you think Jonathan had in mind?"

"A quick touch — for turning up the letters. You offered me fifteen thousand. He might have raised that by ten."

He brushed a finger at his mustache. "I don't know," he said. "In a case like this, he wouldn't have left it to chance. He wouldn't have relied on me to get in touch with him. Three weeks have already gone by. If he had wanted in — he could have arranged to be the go-between. He could have forced himself into the situation."

"That's occurred to me too."

"What do you think?"

"I don't know. You're the guy that says he uses a rapier rather than a bludgeon. Up to now, it's been strictly bludgeon."

"And completely unlike him."

"You think there's more than just the blackmail?"

"Yes, I do."

"So do I."

The man came with the checkbook and the pen. Aldridge wrote a check — to me — for fifteen thousand dollars. I looked at it. I said, "It should be fourteen. You've already paid me one."

"Whose money is it?"

"Yours."

"Let it stand."

I put the check away and the letters. I said, "For a guy booked for murder, you're taking it real cool."

"I didn't kill him. I've told the truth. I'm not worried in the least. I'm a great believer in the efficiency of the police. They're making a mistake, but they've made mistakes before that have straightened out. But I do wish Warren Dodge got in touch with me. Have you found him yet?"

The guy had enough worries. I said, "No. But we will."

"Will," he said. "Why in heaven's name should anybody force my uncle to change his will in order to enrich *me* . . .?" He brushed his finger at his mustache again, ran the finger up along his cheek and dug it into his temple.

Suddenly, I knew where I was going. I said, "Do you happen to know the phone number of Dodge's secretary? Mamie . . ."

"As a matter of fact, I do. Mamie Miller. Lives with her sister. Let me think now." He closed his eyes, remembering, then he gave me the number.

Parker came to us. "Okay," he said. "We break it up now."

Downstairs, I called Mamie. I asked her to meet me in the lobby of the Flatiron Building, it was important. I hung up and called Jonathan Nolan. He wasn't home.

13.

Mamie took me up to Dodge's office. We put on the lights and I went into the library. I said, "I'm going to do a little studying."

"Studying? Here?" She sounded bewildered. "Why?"

"Because there's a law library here. I'm playing a hunch. I'm bouncing bludgeons against rapiers, and playing a hunch."

"Hunch?" she said.

"In my business, it's part of the standard equipment. Hunch, sixth sense, experience, unconscious urge — it's got a lot of names, and none of them actually makes sense."

"Bludgeons?" she said. "And rapiers?"

"Figure of speech. In a cockeyed kind of way, I'm trying to get the guy that got Mr. Dodge."

That made her happier.

I said, "How is he?"

"I call the hospital each hour. So far, each time, the report is 'Fair.' "

"Could be worse," I said.

She said, "Yes. I'll go outside now and let you work."

I pored over books like a kid giving a workout to pornography. I knew what I was looking for, and I knew where to look, but this wasn't my racket, and it took time. I got close a couple of times, but not close enough. I checked each reference and the books piled up on the library table like a football heap on an autumn gridiron and then — bang — I had it right on the head. I closed the book and folded it under my arm and went out to Mamie. I said, "Okay, Sweetie, we can blow the joint now."

"Blow?" she said. "Joint?"

"I'll take you home now, and thanks for the use of the hall. And I'm borrowing this law book."

Dear old Mamie. She said, "Oh. You'll have to sign a receipt." She sat down at the typewriter and tapped out a receipt that had more clauses than Donald Root's will. I signed it, and she put out the lights, and we got out of there, and downstairs I shoved two fingers into my mouth and shrilled for a cab.

I took Mamie home first, and then I had the cabbie drive me to 35th Street, and we stopped at a cafeteria, and he waited while I went in and used a public phone and called Nolan, and got no answer. Mr. Nolan was out having himself a good time, but he wasn't going to have a good time for long. I went back to the cab and said, "10 West 35th."

It turned out to be a four-story house with a re-modeled front, an open downstairs door, and no elevators inside. I trudged up two flights to 2E, rang the bell for just-in-case, and then used Mel's key to invite myself in. I flipped a light and locked the door behind me. I laid down the law book and did quick exploring. There were three rooms: a bedroom with an extra wide bed, an ample kitchen, and a large living room with good furniture, a liquor cabinet with a lot of bottles, and high bookcases along the walls with a preponderance of law books. I moved a chair so that it faced the door, switched off the lights, sat down, and let myself get angry.

I didn't smoke. I didn't want him to open his door and get a whiff of tobacco. I sat very still and grew rigid, waiting. I thought about a son of a bitch who used a girl for a patsy and put her in a spot where she could do time for attempted extortion. I thought about a burning cigar thrown at the face of a stranger. I thought about a guy grabbing a fallen man's hair and rapping the back of his head against a stone floor. I thought about the back end of a heater crashing into the skull of a man past seventy. I thought about murder, putting a bullet into the head of an invalid trapped in a wheel chair . . . and then there were footfalls in the corridor outside the door, and a key in the lock, and I was standing up, waiting for a guy that was good with his mitts, that had been an amateur champion and a professional pug, a guy with big shoulders and a lot of power, and a guy that would stop at nothing.

The door opened and I hit him.

The left caught him in the stomach, and he bent over face forward, and the right caught him with all my strength square on the nose, and I could hear the break of bone under the impact of the blow. But he didn't go down. He rushed me and kicked his knee hard to my groin, and I fell against him, and we both fell against the door, closing it. We struggled against the closed door, his knees punching up viciously, always toward my groin. It was too dark to see, but I didn't stop swinging, and then a fist caught me on the point of the chin, and I flew back and fell to the floor.

He clicked on the light.

I could see him coming at me now. He plunged forward at me in a flying leap, and yet, in one second, you notice the craziest things. At the very moment that you see the blood on his face and his nose blue and twisted, you notice too that he's wearing the same suit as yesterday, and you see the watch chain across his vest and the dangling gold boxing glove. He was flying toward me, but the heel of my shoe cracked against his eye, and he fell sidewise, and now I was on top of him, a knee in his belly and my fists rapping at his face. But he was strong, and somehow, his hands came up and clutched at my throat, and his thumbs pressed in against my Adam's apple, and I wheezed for breath and I fell off him, but I twisted out of the grip of his hands.

He was up now, near the liquor cabinet. He grabbed at the neck of a bottle, smashed off the base against a corner of the cabinet, and he was coming at me, the ragged-edged bottle a murderous weapon. I was on one knee, like a runner starting for a sprint. He came at me, and I jumped, and I caught the wrist of the hand holding the bottle, and we struggled again, panting, tight to each other, the jagged bottle waving above us, a weapon of many daggers. Sweat popped from both of us, and hand trembled against wrist, and then I swept the hand down and the bottle slashed at his ear, and it slit the ear where it was attached to the head, and the blood came down in a red sheet, and it must have frightened him, because the grip on the bottle loosened, and I shook it out of his hand, and it fell to the floor crashing to pieces. He turned, just as I wheeled, and my left caught him on the nose again, in a full pivot, and he stood still, like a stricken animal, shaking his head. I had him down to size now. He ripped open his jacket, and I saw the holster, and he was fumbling for a gun, but he didn't have a chance. It was like chopping down a tree. I kept banging fists at his face until my arms were tired, and then he stumbled, and he fell flat on his back, spread-eagled and unconscious, blood gurgling from his mouth.

I leaned against a wall and waited for the fire to go out of my lungs. Then I went to him, and bent to him, and looked at each end of the watch chain and found what I expected. One vest pocket held a watch, the other a sharp gold knife. The knife sparkled clean — Mr. Nolan had done a good job of cleansing — but nothing was going to help him. I reached into my own pocket for the tuft of red carpet out of Donald Root's apartment. If a clincher was going to be necessary, this would be the clincher. I tucked the tuft deep into the knife pocket, returned the knife, put the watch back in the other pocket, stood up and went to the phone. For the second time in two days I called my doctor in an emergency, but this was someone else's emergency. I got through to him and I said, "Doc?"

"Yes?"

"Pete Chambers. I need you bad. Emergency."

"If it's an emergency . . ."

"It's an emergency. 10 West 35th. Apartment 2E. As fast as possible. Brother, am I going to get a bill this month."

"Brother, you're not kidding."

Nolan slumbered raspingly as I

made more phone calls. I called Anabel and I told her to come a-visiting and to come quickly. Then I called Parker at Headquarters. I said, "I've got your murderer."

"Which murderer?"

"Donald Root."

"Wrong number. *I've* got that murderer."

"No, you haven't. Come on up here."

"Where?"

"Jonathan Nolan's apartment. 10 West 35th. 2E."

"That the other nephew?"

"That's right."

"We've been trying to contact him."

"I've got him for you. Right here."

"See you."

"The faster the better."

While I waited I eavesdropped on Roger Aldridge's correspondence. You think of Roger Aldridge, prim with blue grey temples and a white mustache and an affected enunciation, and you read the incandescent letters that show the man inside the man, and it gives you a chuckle.

I built a bonfire in an ashtray and burned the letters and opened a window and flicked the ashes to oblivion. Then the bell was ringing. It was Doc with his little black bag. He saw his patient at once, opened his bag, and went to work on him. "What happened to this guy?" he murmured. "Get his head caught in a concrete mixer?"

"Search me?" I said.

"Yeah," Doc said. "Search you." He kept working.

I said, "How is he?"

"Pretty bad."

He stitched his eye, took four sutures bringing the ear back to the face, and stuffed plugs into a nostril.

I said, "He come to yet?"

"He's semi-conscious." He took a hypo out of his bag.

I said, "What are you going to do?"

"Give him a jab."

"I want him conscious, Doc."

"He'll be conscious, but woozy."

"Woozy's all right with me, as long as he stays with us and knows what's going on."

Doc said, "Give me a hand."

We lifted him to a couch and Doc gave him the needle.

Then the bell was ringing again, and our first visitor was Anabel Jolly in a mauve suit and glistening nylons and mauve shoes and a black net blouse right up to the neck, and then Parker piled in with a pair of burly cops.

I pointed at the couch. I said, "There's your murderer."

Nolan leaned on one elbow and observed us groggily.

Parker glanced at the patched-up face, said, "What happened to him?"

"Concrete mixer," Doc said.

Parker said, succinctly: "Uh-huh."

"The bullet in the ceiling," I

said. "That gave it to me right away. I don't care how hard you tried to convince me, Lieutenant, you weren't happy with that bullet in the ceiling."

Parker said, "If you've got a story, let's have it."

"Miss Jolly's got a story first."

"Who's Miss Jolly?"

"The lady over there. You've got the floor, Anabel."

Miss Jolly told her story.

"That," said Parker, "implicates him in a blackmail deal. It doesn't make him out a murderer. He was looking for a big touch, and a fast one."

"Wrong," I said.

"Why?"

"Because that's with a bludgeon. This guy makes with a rapier."

Parker squinted his eyes. "What? What's that?"

"This guy's complex. The blackmail deal was to provide a motive for Roger Aldridge. Exactly what you fell for. All of a sudden, Aldridge needed two hundred and fifty thousand dollars. And he needed it bad. A partnership in Winston Parnell was at stake."

"Let's have the story," Parker said. "*Your* way."

"Nolan knew that Aldridge didn't have that kind of loot. He knew that sooner or later, he'd appeal to Donald Root. So he kept an eye on him, and today, when Aldridge finally went to Root, Nolan was his tail. He had this on him." I went to Nolan, opened his jacket, took the gun out of the holster, and gave it to Parker. "Exhibit One," I said.

Parker fondled the gun. "Go on."

"Nolan knew that Emerson Beach was off. He knew that Beach was due back at five. Nolan is a nephew, knew all about the old man's habits. So . . . as close to five as he dared, he rang the bell, ducked when Aldridge answered, then jumped him and blasted him with the butt end of the heater."

"That way," Parker said, "going along with your story, Aldridge couldn't identify his assailant."

"Correct. He knew that Aldridge carried a gun. We'll suppose, of course, he wore gloves. He took out Aldridge's gun, threatened the old man, got the will out of the safe where it was kept, and had the old man change it . . . under threat of death. This done, he plugged the old man. With Aldridge's gun. Then he put the gun in Aldridge's hand, and shot another bullet. The one in the ceiling."

This time it was Doc who asked the question: "Why?"

"To get cordite impregnations in Aldridge's hand. These show up in a thing called the paraffin gauntlet test. The Lieutenant understands."

Parker said, "Yeah."

"Then he turned him around to face the door, as though he was on his way out. Then he cut a slit in the carpet to make it look as though it had torn when Aldridge supposedly tripped on it. Then he scuffed it wide with the point of Aldridge's shoe, stuck the point in, and now it looked like Aldridge tripped and knocked himself out in his hurry to scram. He had to work fast. He wanted Aldridge still unconscious when Beach returned."

"Any idea," Parker said, "what he used to cut this alleged slit?"

I went near to Nolan. "He wears this watch chain." I reached in for the knife attached to the chain. "This, Lieutenant, is a knife. And it looks like it's recently been carefully cleaned." I dug into the pocket, and then, surprise, surprise, I came up with a tuft of red carpet. "But I think, Lieutenant, that he forgot to clean the pocket."

This was evidence. The Lieutenant alerted to action. He grabbed the tuft of carpet, examined it, took a piece of paper out of his pocket, folded it into the paper, and put the paper away. "Anything else?" he said.

"Plenty else. He was through, and he wanted to get out fast, away from the scene of action. He had rigged his plant and he wanted out. He knew nothing of the fact that I was due there, and Warren Dodge. He knew Beach was due, and he wanted to duck out. But as the elevator came down, he saw Warren Dodge in the lobby. Dodge had his back to him. It wouldn't do for Dodge to see him there, it wouldn't do at all. So out came the heater, and he opened Dodge's skull with it. It took eleven stitches."

"Where's Dodge now?"

"At the Flower Hospital. He'll give you a full statement the minute you fix him up with the facts."

"But if he had his back turned, how'd he see him?"

"He was facing a mirror. He saw him, but he couldn't get out of the way in time. That's positive evidence, Lieutenant."

To Nolan, Parker said, "Can you talk?"

"I can talk," Nolan said.

"Any remarks?"

"Strictly a frame."

Grimly Parker said, "It's a frame you're going to punch hard to get out of."

"Where's motive?" Nolan said. "I wouldn't kill Root to make Roger richer. You may be able to hold me, Lieutenant, but a jury'll throw you out of Court."

Parker turned to me. "He's got a point there."

"No, he hasn't."

"Why?"

"Because I can show you motive. This is a shrewdie. He works both ends against the middle. It only *looks* like no motive."

"Show me," Parker said.

"You know that Nolan is the only other heir at law of Donald Root."

"So?"

"Where's the will?"

Parker produced it.

"Notice," I said, "that the additional bequest is written *after* the signature."

"I also notice that the bequest is to Aldridge, not Nolan."

"Hold it," I said. I went to the law book and opened it to the place I had marked. "My reference," I said in my best lawyer-like tones, "is to a case entitled In Re Ryan's Will, 252 N. Y. 620. Therein we have a rule of law. *A will is void when not signed at its physical end.* Thus, if after the signature, there is more writing of a dispository nature, the will is not signed at its physical end, and it is therefore void in its entirety. That's the law."

The Lieutenant scratched his head. "Sure," he said. "If the will is void, Donald Root dies intestate. Intestate — which means without a will — then his heirs at law inherit. That cuts Nolan in for half."

"Very good, Lieutenant." I snapped the book shut.

The Lieutenant beckoned one of the officers. "Nippers," he said in his politest tone, "for Mr. Nolan."

The officer grinned and complied. Nolan was finished. I wasn't.

"Just in case that wouldn't work," I said, "there's another rule of law."

Parker beamed. "Hidden talents," he said. "A real legal eagle."

"There's a rule of law that states that a criminal cannot profit by his own wrongdoing. Thus, if Nolan's plant worked, Aldridge would be convicted of the murder . . . which covered Nolan two ways. First, if the will were declared void, then the entire estate would go to the heirs. Since Aldridge could not profit by his own wrongdoing . . . the entire estate would go to one Jonathan Nolan."

"And second?" Parker said.

"If by chance the will would hold up, then the charitable bequest would go to the charity named — but Aldridge's share could not go to Aldridge. Same reason . . . criminal cannot profit by his own wrongdoing. If you'll look, you'll see there is no direction as to what happens with any part of the estate that, for some reason, cannot go as the testator wished. For that share of the estate, then, the testator, Donald Root, is deemed to have no will. And his heir at law inherits. Who dat? Jonathan Nolan again."

"So the worst that could happen to him," Parker said, "is that he winds up with half the estate."

"How's that for motive?"

"Pretty good. And pretty slick."

"Finished?" inquired Anabel Jolly.

"Yes," I said.

"Put the book away."

I put the book away.

She took me under the arm and led me to the door.

Parker called: "Where to, you?"

Jolly smiled. "I'm going to do a little cross-examining on my own."

"Cross-examining?" Parker said.

"He's good at making like a detective, and he's good at talking like a lawyer. Now I want to find out how good he is at ringing bells."

"Bells?" said Parker.

"You heard me, Lieutenant."

She marched me out.

The Watcher

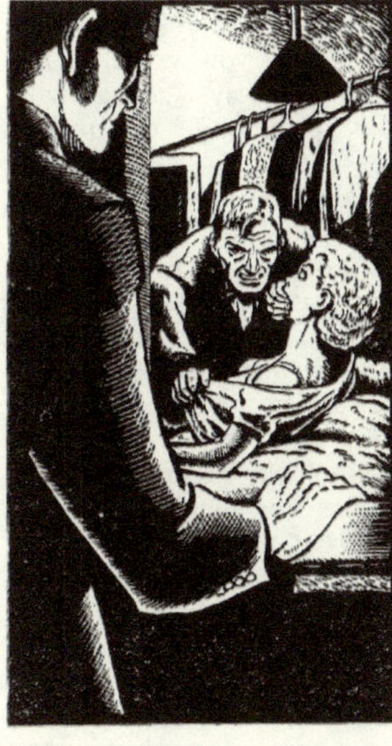

I stood outside and watched the guy grab Marcia. I could have stopped him — but Marcia had it coming.

BY PETER PAIGE

WHEN I glanced through the small alley window and saw two men crowd Marcia Smith into the rear of her tailor shop my first instinct was to step in the alley door and surprise them. A second glance stopped me. The skinny fellow had whirled Marcia around a partition to where they stood alone amid miles of unpressed clothes.

He must have been stronger than he looked. Despite her struggling, one hand pinned her motionless while the other worked her skirt over her hips and sent it to the floor.

I started for the doorway, hesitated.

Let her taste a little of that, I thought. *She's been asking for it a long, long time . . .*

I could always move in and stop it if it went too far.

The mustached fellow was strictly business. He emptied the cash drawer, then shook out her purse on the counter and swept bills and change into his pocket. He seemed oblivious to the struggle raging behind the partition.

The skinny attacker's palm over Marcia's mouth held her jet black hair-do against his chest while his free hand ripped open her blouse in front. With quick, practiced motions he slid it off her shoulders, then jerked down. It came off her hands and fluttered between their feet.

Her eyes over his palm rolled wildly. Her hands clawed to keep her pink bra on — but lost it to a vicious swipe that left red streaks on the white inner slopes of her breasts.

I thought, *good! She's been playing with fire so long — let her burn a little . . .*

Little enough burning for all her teasing ways. To meet me on the street with a nod and a smile and a word was never enough. She had to follow her breasts almost into me, laughing . . . reading my mind and laughing . . . her tongue alive between gleaming teeth and scarlet lips.

She wore tight dresses. Or snug sweaters and free-wheeling skirts. Or fluffy blouses and sleek skirts. All of them leaving her nuder than if she went around naked. She used too much lipstick, too much perfume. Strangers to the neighborhood often followed her into her shop under a mistaken impression.

She had no known boy friend, nor had anyone in the neighborhood ever dated her, to my knowledge. Time and again I tried. Each time, she toyed with the idea. She would grip my biceps, stand close enough for me to feel the tips of her nipples and tilt her head back so I could watch the teasing devils in her large violet eyes. And she would toy with the idea of a date with me.

"After dinner, a show and dancing — what?" she asked one such time. "Are you a taxi wrestler, Jimmy? Or would it be a stand-up struggle in my hallway? Or etchings? I think that would be most fun, Jimmy. If we wound up at your place — looking at etchings."

Her breasts nudged me gently. Below them I could see her hips swaying a little as she teased this image of our date to life.

"You'd have drinks for me, wouldn't you, Jimmy? Don't bother with champagne or bourbon. Brandy!" Her eyes glowed. "I love spiced brandies. They make me want to get up and dance. Not ballroom. Alone. Feeling free. My dress seems to choke me. I slip out of it. Everything seems to choke me. I slip out of everything. Spiced brandy does that to me, Jimmy —"

Her fingers burned into my biceps.

"But you wouldn't rush me; would you, Jimmy? Would you be too impatient? Would you wait . . . until, in my own way . . . naturally . . . I went absolutely out of control . . . ?"

Teasing talk — about a date that didn't happen, wasn't expected to happen. Not just to me. To whatever man got her alone. Even the married fellows. Marcia would heat a man to where he'd lose his head and grab for her. In her shop or out on the street, sooner or later he'd grab — and clutch air. She'd be glancing back across her shoulder, making certain he noticed the full swing of her buttocks as she danced away. And between them would hang her mocking laugh.

There's a stronger name for such girls than "tease". When I called her by it one time, she turned white and said, "Say what you damn please; but don't touch! You hear? I'm a look-all-you-want-but-hands-off girl!"

"What are you saving it for?" I'd choked.

She walked into me until we were practically seared together; laughter back in her voice and eyes. "Maybe you, hard guy. Maybe *you!* I once told you to wait. I'll have to get around to it slowly, Jimmy. Think of that and be patient. Wait . . ."

I waited now, my eye to the small alley window. Watching the dancing frenzy of Marcia's breasts and hips to escape the long fingers leaving bright red trails all over her whiteness. The skinny fellow's eyes bulged over a black-toothed grin that sent saliva down his cheeks.

His buddy kept to the shop's front, methodically searching drawers, shelves, closets. He even fingered pockets in the jackets hanging from overhead racks. Not for him that oft-repeated hoot in the next day's paper: . . . *the robbers overlooked a hiding place containing umpty-ump thousands of dollars* . . .

Turning from him, I watched the silent, desperate dance of Marcia and her grinning assailant. And when his free hand began working on his own clothing I again started for the door — and hesitated again . . .

How is it now, Marcia? Did you turn it on when they entered the front door? Did your eyes flash Skinny a promise? Did you take a deep breath to show him exactly what your eyes promised? Did your hips sway teasingly for him? Did you, perhaps, squeeze his arm, starting this one fire you cannot stop?

Through the small window I watched her eyes screaming over his palm on her mouth. He was bending her back and down. Back and down toward the cushion of unpressed clothing. Her breasts seemed about to burst. Her hips flared out. Her lithe body arched like a sapling in a hundred mile gale.

And then she crumpled. She became a motionless pool of whiteness in the shadows at his feet. He crouched over her.

Now, I thought. But my impulse to charge through the doorway was halted by a flicker of movement shifting my attention to the mustached fellow. He had wandered around the partition. Now he gaped, wide-eyed. As if he had been unaware of the struggle all this time. He looked stunned. Then enraged.

Whatever he said brought his partner up on one knee. I could hear only street noises from my post at the alley window. Their argument waxed in pantomime. The skinny fellow left one hand trailing on Marcia, as if to keep reassuring himself she was there.

Saliva spattered from his face when his partner's palm cracked it. He lurched to his feet — and got the front of his shirt bunched in the mustached fellow's fist. Two more slaps sent saliva spraying east and west. The skinny fellow sagged half to his knees, talking earnestly.

Released, he quickly adjusted his clothing, then allowed himself to be prodded toward the front. Neither of them glanced back toward Marcia, motionless on her couch of unpressed clothes.

They hesitated at the counter to check if the way out was clear, then left my field of vision.

I was near the alley's mouth when they passed, the mustached fellow side-mouthing bitterly, "All I told you was to keep her quiet —"

"I was *keepin'* her quiet, Mike," the other whined back eagerly.

I let them go.

Marcia was still unconscious when I reached her via the alley door. I had difficulty wrenching my gaze from the long trails of searching fingers, scarlet against the pallor of her skin. All she had on were nylons and open-toed black pumps.

I checked the time, reached for the wall phone, hesitated. It was only twelve-thirty. Sam, her greyed presser, took every minute the union allowed him. He wouldn't return from lunch a minute before one. The store was empty. It would probably remain empty. Beyond plate glass windows the street held only an occasional passerby as it basked in noonday glare. Lunch hour all through the neighborhood; kids home from school, mothers feeding them.

I hesitated another moment, then stooped over Marcia, gripped her slender chin gently and leaned down to taste the full sweetness of her lips.

Her eyes fluttered open sleepily. I drew back, watching them flood with the shock of remembrance. They veered about, met mine, froze.

I watched them melt into tears of sudden relief.

"Oh, *Jimmy, Jimmy* —"

I brushed a lock of jet black hair from her eyes.

"Two men, Jimmy," she breathed. "Two horrible men. One of them . . . I think he raped —"

Her effort to sit up came into my palm urging her down. Our eyes held.

"I've waited long enough," I whispered.

She stared with growing incredulity as I made the necessary preparations, then terror leaped into her eyes. Her scream broke on my fist.

The Assistant Medical Examiner arose from his knees alongside the body and searched the circle of faces until he found Captain Black, of Homicide.

"She seems to have been punched, clawed, choked and raped. Offhand, I'd say the choking killed her — about half an hour ago, give or take five minutes. The killer should have her blood under his nails, and underwear stains. I'll detail it after we take her apart in the morgue."

Captain Black scowled at his watch. "Half an hour ago was a quarter of one." He raised the scowl to Sam, the greyed presser, who stared back through tear-filled eyes. "Where were you a quarter of one?"

"Eating," Sam croaked hoarsely. "While this was happening to poor Marcia, I was eating —"

"Where?"

"The Henderson Cafeteria. It's on —"

"He was there, all right, Captain," Sergeant Vincenti cut in. "He spoke with Patrolman Wilson when he left the cafeteria at ten to one. And it wasn't more than a few minutes before he came running back, yelling for Wilson to return to the shop with him. Wilson did, and phoned in from here and hasn't been off the premises a minute since, so I guess old Sam is pretty well alibied, Captain."

"I guess he is," Captain Black said drily. "Wilson," he asked, turning, "is there anything you can add to what the sergeant said?"

"Not a thing, Captain," I said.

The Bells Are Ringing

It didn't make sense. The guy was going to get thirty days, so he shot his way out of the station-house.

A John J. Malone Story

BY CRAIG RICE

IT ISN'T OFTEN that a man gets a chance to live a moment of his life over again and do the right thing where he had once done wrong. This is the story of a man who got such a chance, and paid for it — with his life.

It didn't begin that way, of course. Things never began that way for John J. Malone. He had gone to the Chicago Avenue police station to spring a carnival pitchman caught selling something called Big Chief Mulligan's Magic Mountain Fever Cure without the required legal formalities. And arrived there only to find that the fast-talking carny had sprung himself in the meantime. Talked himself right off the blotter, with the help of a love offering of seven bottles of the magic potion. The desk sergeant, it turned out, was a chronic sufferer from Rocky Mountain fever.

What might have been a total loss was slightly compensated by a bottle of the love offering which Sergeant Delaney generously turned over to Mr. Malone. The little lawyer took one sniff of the stuff and decided to call it due and proper consideration in hand given. After all, he reflected, he had come out of bigger cases with less to show for his labors. He took a swig of the elixir, stuffed the bottle in his hip pocket and was about to step out into the raw March afternoon air again when it happened.

It happened so fast that only later, when he had put together the conflicting accounts of eye witnesses, was Malone able to see the full picture in all its fantastic details.

"I'm not saying it didn't happen," he explained to his secretary when he got back to the office. "All I'm saying is, it's impossible."

Maggie sniffed the air suspiciously and, for half a minute, said nothing, with dramatic emphasis. Then, "Is that what you intend to tell Captain von Flanagan?" she asked. "He's called you twice already."

"Von Flanagan? What does *he* want?"

"What does *he* want? You were present at the scene of the crime, weren't you? You're a witness."

"I was under the desk, with Sergeant Delaney and the waste basket," Malone said. "All I know is —"

The telephone rang.

"You answer it, and if it's von Flanagan tell him I was buried this morning, deeply mourned by friends at Joe the Angel's bar —"

Maggie picked up the receiver, held it ten inches from her ear to protect her eardrums, and passed it to Malone, saying, "Here, you take it. This is no language fit for a lady."

"And furthermore," von Flanagan was shouting, "the fugitive is your client. I have it from — Malone, Malone, are you there?"

Malone allowed the better part of a minute to go by while he ceremoniously unwrapped a fresh cigar and lit it. By this time von Flanagan had exhausted the genealogical vagaries of Malone's family tree and was laying down the law of accessory before, during and after the fact.

"Your honor," Malone spoke up at last, putting an edge of sarcasm on his words, "if the court please —"

The voice at the other end of the wire sputtered out in a string of oaths.

"If the court please, your honor," Malone repeated, "I did *not* see what happened, having suddenly been called away by urgent business — under the sergeant's desk. And the guy was *not* my client."

"Don't give me that, Malone. What were you doing at the Chicago Avenue Station this afternoon if it wasn't — I have it from Sergeant Delaney himself —"

"I was there in the interests of a certain medical discovery, Big Chief Mulligan's Magic Mountain Fever Cure —"

Von Flanagan's voice was suddenly grave, almost mournful. "Malone, you've been drinking again?"

"Only what is needful to take the chill out of my bones brought on by a return of my old Rocky Mountain fever," Malone replied. "And as for Sergeant Delaney, he knows I never set eyes on the accused before in my life and I wouldn't know him again if I saw him. Hell, I don't even know his name."

"His name is John Drew and he assaulted an officer, and that is a criminal offense under the laws and statutes of the County of Cook, State of Illinois, and the fugitive was your client and it's your duty to produce him on pain of contempt of court, resisting arrest, harboring a fugitive, accessory after the fact, and I'll throw the switch myself personally at your *own* execution so help me if you don't —"

And that was how it all began. An utter stranger, John Drew by name, had been picked up for disorderly conduct growing out of a brawl in a saloon near Navy Pier, and when Sergeant Delaney ordered him locked up for questioning he had yanked a gun out of the arresting officer's holster and shot his way out of the police station, seriously wounding one of the policemen. "Don't stop me," he had cried out in a voice that was more like a plea than a threat. "Please don't stop me or I'll have to shoot!"

Malone shook his head as he looked across the desk at Maggie. "I don't understand it. It just doesn't make sense. Here was a guy, all he could have got was thirty days in the Bridewell, and what does he do? Shoots a man, a cop at that, just to save himself a night in the lock-up and maybe a few weeks in the clink. I wonder why. I just can't help wondering why."

He took the bottle of Rocky Mountain Fever Cure from his hip pocket and administered the prescribed dose to himself, by mouth, as directed on the label. Then he got up and put on his hat. At the door he paused and turned back to Maggie.

Maggie shook her head. "No, there isn't any money. The rent check went out this morning, remember? But if this will do any good —" She took a five dollar bill from her purse and handed it to Malone.

"Thanks," Malone said. "Be sure and make a note of it. And if von Flanagan calls again tell him my last words were: Crime does not pay — enough."

From Harry Reutlinger at the Chicago *Herald-American* Malone learned that John Drew had been identified as a World War II veteran . . . South Pacific theater of war . . . dishonorable discharge . . . last known address, 3127 Cottage Grove Avenue. "That'll be a lot of help to you," Harry said. "The guy shoots a policeman and then goes quietly home to bed. Anyway, the cops have probably been there already." Just the same Malone jotted down the address. Any guy who was crazy enough to trade a night in the hoosegow for a possible date with the hot seat was nutty enough to do anything.

Thirty-one-twenty-seven Cottage Grove Avenue turned out to be an old deserted house, windows boarded up, door hanging limp on one hinge. Probably hadn't been lived in for years, Malone thought. He took a look at the meter ticking away and decided to take the streetcar back. No use running up the investment. He dismissed the cab and, since there was no car in sight yet, decided to have a look around before leaving. Hunches are like fish stories. The ones you hear about are the ones that happen to pan out. If this one failed to pan out, well, no one but himself would ever know about it.

It was dark in there, the only light being the light that came in from the street lamp through the cracks in the boarded-up windows. The floors creaked and the wallpaper hung down from the walls in ribbons. Malone was just about to leave when he heard something. He stopped, holding his breath, listening. It was footsteps. And then a voice out of the darkness, a voice he recognized as the voice he had heard pleading, "Don't stop me!" at the Chicago Avenue police station just before the fatal shooting. But this time it was not a pleading voice. From the tone of it he could have guessed, if he didn't already know, that it was backed up by the authority of a .38 caliber police revolver.

"Don't move. I've got a gun."

"I wouldn't brag about it, Drew. Not the way *you* got it," Malone said.

"So you know my name," the voice replied. "Who are you?"

"John J. Malone, counselor and attorney-at-law. Captain Daniel von Flanagan of Homicide has taken it into his head that I'm the attorney of record for the defense in your case, so I've come here to talk it over. But the first thing I want to know, Drew — why did you come back here? You know this is the first place the cops are sure to look for you."

"They've been here and gone," Drew said. "I saw them, tramping all over the place, only they didn't see me. I was watching them from a window across the street. The way I figure it, the safest place to be is where the cops have been — and gone."

"That adds up to a good deal of sense," Malone said. "You know something, Drew? You're smart. How come you do a crazy thing like shooting your way out of a disorderly rap that couldn't have gotten you more than a few days in the clink? You're lucky you didn't kill that cop, but they aren't passing out any medals for bad marksmanship. Why did you do it, Drew?"

"Why should I tell you?"

"Because von Flanagan has taken it into his fool head that I'm your lawyer. Here's my card." He took a step forward but Drew stopped him, quickly.

"Take one step more and I'll

shoot!" Then, in a voice that sounded once more like the pleading voice in the police station, "I didn't want to hurt that policeman, and I don't want to hurt you, but so help me, if you take one more step —"

"Okay," Malone said, "but you're going to have to tell it to someone, sooner or later. Besides, there's that court martial during the war, in the South Pacific —"

"So you know about that, too?'

"You were court martialed," Malone went on, "and handed a dishonorable discharge. Maybe you'll tell 'me *that* was a raw deal, a bum rap. Was that what soured you on the world, and made you determined to get even with society?"

He must have touched a raw nerve that time, Malone decided. For a minute Drew nearly lost control of his trigger finger. "I ought to have more sense than to stand here gabbing with you," he growled. "I ought to shoot you like I shot the cop, and clear out of here. And this time I ain't gonna miss."

He paused, as if he were turning the idea over in his mind. Malone's feet seemed to be rooted to the spot. Drops of sweat poured down his face and tickled the side of his nose, but he wasn't laughing. There wasn't anything funny about those cold eyes watching him in the semi-darkness. Nor about the cold glint of that gun barrel staring him in the face.

"All right," he said, "so the army gave you a raw deal. Then why not tell me about it? I'm your lawyer. I'm giving you a chance to tell your side of the story."

"Why should I?" Drew replied. "Nobody'll believe me. Nobody believed me then, and nobody'll believe me now. Besides, you'll never live to tell it, anyway."

"So what have you got to lose?" Malone said.

As a lawyer Malone had found out one thing: few people can resist the temptation to tell their side of a story. Especially if they feel they've been wronged. Especially if they've been carrying the story around in their hearts for years, like John Drew, with no one to listen, no one willing to believe.

As John Drew poured out his story Malone felt himself transported suddenly to the steaming foxholes of a South Pacific island. The Cottage Grove Avenue car going by outside sounded like the rattle of Jap machine guns, spitting death out of the jungle night.

It was a story of one of war's many grotesque horrors, a story of terror, and fear. Days without rest, nights without sleep, and a wounded buddy lying out there in no-man's land, hanging there on the barbed wire and gasping out his last heart-rending cries for help. To John Drew fell the task of crawling out under covering fire and bringing in the wounded man.

"How can I tell you what it was like? That voice, those screams out there in the night, and me rooted to the ground like in a nightmare, unable to move a muscle. . . . Well, in the morning they found the both of us. The wounded man, my buddy, still hanging on the barbed-wire . . . dead. And me, crouching in a hole in the ground, less than fifty feet away . . . not a mark on me." He paused, and a heavy sigh filled the silence. "What else is there to tell? They brought me up for court martial. 'Why did you take cover and let a wounded comrade die without offering assistance, contrary to orders?' 'Because he didn't *deserve* to live,' I told them. 'What do you mean the wounded man didn't deserve to live?' 'I can't tell you,' I told them. 'What do you mean? You won't tell us?' 'All right, I *won't* tell you.'

"That did it. They threw the book at me. One year in prison for disobedience to orders, insubordination, I don't know what all. I served my time, and when it was over I came back . . . just drifting around, one place and another . . . trying to pull myself together, and make a fresh start."

"Why didn't you tell them, Drew, when they asked you?"

"What was the use? They wouldn't have understood."

"Now listen to me, Drew," Malone said gently. "I *will* try to understand. Why didn't the wounded man deserve to live? Was it some wrong he'd done you?"

His answer startled Malone.

"He was a new man in the outfit. I never saw him before in my life. I didn't even know his name."

"Then how did you know he didn't deserve to live?"

For the first time Drew's voice rose, and now there was anguish in it. Anguish and defiance.

"Because *nobody* deserves to live! Because . . . if *she* can't live, *nobody* deserves to live. Not the man on the barbed wire, nor the policeman I killed, nor you, nor me . . . nobody's got a right to live if *she* isn't allowed to live."

Who was *she?* Malone started to ask that question when the sound of police sirens came from the distance. Suddenly Drew was alert, once more the hunted man.

"Get down on the floor!" he ordered. "And if I hear one sound out of you I'll shoot!"

Keeping the little lawyer covered with the gun Drew moved over to the window and looked out through a crack between the boards.

"They're back," he whispered. "They've decided to come back and search the other houses on the block."

Malone could hear voices now, and knocking on doors, as the police went from house to house in search of the fugitive. Once they stopped in front of the deserted house, debating whether they ought to search the old house again. Malone held his breath, wondering if he could take a chance and cry out, but Drew was standing over him, the gun pointed straight at his head.

The voices grew dim, and presently the sound of the sirens died away in the distance. And Malone realized he was alone in a deserted house with a madman who might take it into his head any minute that he, Malone, didn't deserve to live, any more than the policeman at the station, or the man on the barbed wire. What have I got to lose? he asked himself, and when he saw Drew move away to have another look out the window he jumped him, aiming for the gun hand.

For a while it was nip and tuck as they rolled over the creaking floor together in a death struggle for possession of the weapon. Malone kept his grip on the wrist till Drew was finally forced to drop the gun and then he pounced on it.

Now that the tables were turned Drew was a changed man. Gone was the air of defiance, and in its place was a pitiful pleading.

"I could have killed you, and I didn't. I gave *you* a chance. Now listen to *me*."

"I'll listen to you," Malone said, "if you'll tell me one thing. Who was *she*?"

Drew's face in the half light looked to Malone like the faces of men he'd seen in the death house, just before they made their last confession.

Drew had loved a girl. Joan was her name, and she was as beautiful as she was good. The soul of generosity and human warmth. Loved by all who knew her. He and Joan — their love was like something the evil fates had forgotten to destroy in a world where everything that was good, everything that was beautiful and generous and kind, was being destroyed in the fires of war and hate. Then suddenly, like a bird stricken on the wing, Joan was taken ill. The doctors said it was T.B., and she was taken to a sanatorium.

"I offered to marry her anyway, but I guess my heart wasn't in it, and she seemed to sense it. 'I'll always feel you did it because you pitied me,' she said. I should have insisted, but I didn't. I guess I've always been a coward that way, afraid, running away from something. My visits to the sanatorium became less and less frequent. Then came Pearl Harbor. That gave me the excuse I wanted. I went off to the South Pacific, trying to forget, but the guilt kept gnawing at my insides. It wouldn't let me sleep. I had deserted her. . . .

"I kept telling myself, 'It isn't *your* fault. It's life. Life just didn't give her an even break.' And then the thought came to me: if life didn't give her a chance to live, then *nobody* deserved to live!

"That's what I was thinking when I tried to crawl out to the barbed wire that night. Joan was everything that was good and beautiful and true. If Joan couldn't live what right did *he* have to live? What right did anybody have?"

Malone said, "That explains why you got yourself in a jam with the court martial, but I still can't see why you had to go and shoot that policeman today."

"I came back from the Pacific," Drew went on. "I drifted from town to town. Last week I came back here. It was a struggle but I finally got up the courage to go and see Joan. The doctor said it was only a matter of days, but he hadn't told her, and she seemed to think she was getting better. 'It won't be long now,' she said, 'and I'll be going out of here.' Then it came to me in a flash. This was my chance, my second chance, to do something I should have done long ago. 'I love you, Joan,' I said, 'I've always loved you. I want you to marry me.'

"This time she said yes, and we set the date.

"And now you know why I had to get away from there, why I couldn't let *anything* detain me," Drew said, and there was a note of bitter irony in his voice. "Tomorrow is my wedding day."

So *that* was it. One decent thing in a lifetime of being afraid and running away. One last chance to make good, to prove to himself that he could be like other men. That he could face life and do his duty like a man. That was what he wanted.

Malone turned the thing over in his mind. What should he do? What *could* he do? Half the cops in the county prowling the streets in search of John Drew, an armed fugitive. All he had to do was put one foot out the door and he'd be shot down like a dog in the streets. And here he was, babbling like a madman about getting married tomorrow. The sensible thing to do was to march him straight off to the nearest patrol box and put in a call for the police. The little lawyer looked towards the window and through the cracks he could see that the dawn was beginning to break. The dawn of John Drew's wedding day.

"Okay," he said. "You're going to get your chance — if we can get out of here and to the sanatorium before the cops pick us *both* up. And when it's over you'll give yourself up immediately to the police."

It wasn't easy slipping out of that abandoned house and over the miles of city and countryside to the remote and isolated private sanatorium. Malone knew he was sticking his neck out, aiding a fugitive to evade justice, even if only for a little while. And if they caught up with him and Drew, would they wait for him to explain? A warning of what awaited them was sounded only a few minutes after they had slipped out of the house through a rear exit and by way of the alley into a neighbor's back yard. Through a kitchen window it came to them, blaring out of the radio —

"Attention! Attention, everybody! The assailant of Policeman Emmet Nelson is still at large. Citizens are warned to be on the lookout for a man about thirty years of age, medium height, black hair and swarthy complexion, grey suit, khaki shirt, no tie, brown army brogues. This man is armed. Police have been ordered to approach with caution. If resistance is offered, shoot to kill."

"You hear that!" Drew said. "They're not going to give me a chance. Give me that gun."

"Now listen to me, Drew," Malone said. "*I've* got the gun and I mean to keep it. Don't be a fool. If you keep your head and do as I tell you I'll see you through this." To himself he was saying: I'd better have a story ready for von Flanagan, and it better be a good one.

They had reached the end of the alley and stood waiting for a chance to slip out into the street. Footsteps sounded hollow, echoing along the street, and they slunk back into the shadows, waiting. It was only a mechanic in overalls going to work, swinging his lunch box and whistling a tune as he passed on his way to the street car stop.

"We can't risk taking a street car," Malone said, "We'll have to hail a cab." It seemed forever till a Yellow came into view and when it did they had to scurry for cover again to avoid being spotted by a police prowl car. The strain was beginning to tell on Drew. He was breathing hard.

"Why can't we steal a car —"

"That's out," Malone said. "One crime at a time, that's *my* motto."

"We could hitch a ride," Drew said.

"And if the driver recognizes you?"

"We've got a gun —"

"*I've* got a gun," Malone corrected him, "and don't you forget it. The prowl car is gone now. Let's get moving."

How they ever succeeded in eluding the police that morning Malone was never able to explain afterwards. The streets seemed to be swarming with them. Most of the way they made it on foot, through alleys and across vacant lots. At a roadside telephone booth Malone stopped to put in a call to Captain von Flanagan, to meet him at the sanatorium. And hung up before the flabbergasted von Flanagan could ask him why. For the last mile or two they managed to flag down a taxi.

"What do you know about that waterfront rat shootin' down a cop," the cabby remarked over his shoulder. "Right in the police station, too. He must be nuts." And, a few minutes later, "Hey, you know something? I wouldn't give you a plugged nickel for that guy's life right now."

Malone was watching Drew's face. He had seen faces like that. In the death cell. Doomed men, yet strangely at peace, ready for the last mile.

Yes, the last mile. Journey's end. Handing the taxi driver his fare Malone felt like he was paying off the executioner.

Inside the sanatorium they found

everything in readiness. Flowers, music, guests. The minister waiting. In this isolated place nobody had heard as yet about the shooting in which John Drew was involved. Malone said nothing, watching Drew, his hand in his coat poket, finger on the trigger. It relaxed only for a minute as he looked down at the girl on the hospital bed, as beautiful as any bride on her wedding day, her cheeks flushed with the deceptive flush of the dying T.B. victim. The doctor turned to Malone.

"It's only a matter of hours now," he whispered. "She'll never last out the day."

The minister began the marriage ceremony.

"Dearly beloved, we are gathered together here in the sight of God, and in the face of this company, to join together this man and this woman in holy matrimony. . . ."

Malone heard the words as if they came from far away, like words in a dream.

". . . which is an honorable estate, instituted by God. . . ."

As the music died away on the last notes of "O, Promise Me," it was mingled with the wail of the siren outside announcing the arrival of Captain von Flanagan and the men of Homicide.

Malone looked at John Drew and Drew nodded back.

"Let's go," Drew said.

Case History

BY CHARLES BECKMAN, JR.

The letters got worse and worse. Evelyn had to stop them — and that was how Nick came into the case.

I WORK a private detective agency with my brother, Tim. Sometimes we get some screwy cases. This Evelyn Rose thing, for example. I've got it all down in this private record book I keep. If you've got a minute, I'll run through it for you. . . .

May 10

Got to the office late. Tim had left a message for me. "Go see an Evelyn Rose at 365-C Chambers Drive."

I piled in the coupe and drove over to the address. It turned out to be a big brick apartment building on a shaded street, surrounded by a lot of other similar buildings. I pressed a buzzer and walked upstairs to apartment "C." In a few minutes the door opened. What looked out shouldn't happen to a poor, low-income bachelor.

She had red hair, but not everyday, run-of-the-mill red hair. If you filled a tub with burgundy and looked into the deep, maroon depths with the light striking it just right, you might get the shade I'm talking about. As if that luscious dark red mop wasn't enough, nature had also endowed her with flawless, cream-white skin. All of this loveliness was encased in green silk lounging pajamas that kind of slithered and writhed around her curves.

"Yes?" she asked. Her pretty aquamarine eyes looked half-awake, as if she'd rolled around most of the night and finally taken a handful of sleeping pills.

"Nick Scotch, Ma'am, of the Scotch Detective Agency. You called our office today and asked us to send out a man, I believe?"

"Oh." She looked at me and blinked. She pushed the tumbling red hair away from her left eye. The movement made the light flash on what was at least a three-carat diamond on the third finger of her left hand. "Won't you come in, Mr. Scotch?"

It was a pleasure, believe me.

As I followed her, I noted the refinement in her posture. She was in her late twenties. Her voice was beautifully modulated, cultured. A guy like me could look and dream, but that's all. She was strictly out of my class. College, exclusive finishing school, a trip or two to Europe, then a carefully supervised engagement and a substantial marriage. That was, no doubt, her background, tied up in one neat bundle.

The apartment was tastefully done in modern furniture. Mrs. Rose indicated a chair and disappeared into another room. She returned very shortly with a drink in either hand. She gave me one of them and then sat on the couch, curling her legs under her. She pushed that burgundy hair back again and lit a cigarette. I noticed that her fingers trembled a bit when she pulled an ash tray closer.

Sometimes you've got to break the ice a little with the nervous ones. I asked, politely, "What seems to be the trouble, Mrs. Rose?"

She inhaled deeply, blew the smoke out as if she were trying to put out a candle. She picked a minute particle of tobacco off her carmine lips and put the cigarette in the ash tray. Then she changed her mind and picked it up again. "It's horrible," she said. "I must stop it somehow or I shall lose my mind. How much do you charge, Mr. Scotch?"

Before I had a chance to correlate any of these disjointed sentences and come up with an answer, she started talking again. "It's been going on for weeks now, Mr. Scotch. I'm so worried I'm nearly out of my mind." She started crying. Her throat worked and she put her hands shakily over her eyes. "These terrible, nasty letters and things. . . ."

I made a sympathetic sound. "Maybe if you can give me the details, Mrs. Rose, I can help you."

"Yes." She put out her cigarette jerkily, got up from the couch and left the room. It was something to see, that woman walking out of a room in those clinging silk pajamas. If she had anything on under them, my eyes were out of focus.

She came back with a bundle of envelopes held together with a rubber band. She dropped them in my lap as if they were covered with some kind of revolting fungus. "I haven't any business keeping them, Mr. Scotch. I threw the first ones away, naturally. But when they kept coming I thought I'd better save them to show a detective agency." She went over and plopped back down on the couch and nervously worried the cellophane off a fresh package of cigarettes. The top of her pajamas had worked out of the bottoms, disclosing a portion of her slim, white middle.

With an effort, I concentrated on the packet of mail. I pulled the top envelope out of the bundle. "Do you want me to see this, Mrs. Rose?"

"Yes." She blushed. "It's awfully embarrassing, but I guess you must, if you're going to help me."

I took a sheet of paper out of the envelope. "Darling," the typewritten words said, "I made believe you were beside me last night. The moonlight was coming through the window, falling all over you. You didn't have any clothes on at all. Then you —" I stopped reading. A dull flush came up over my shirt collar.

"They get worse," she said grimly. "That's one of the tamest ones. Some of the envelopes have other . . . things in them. You know, intimate, personal things, and some horrible drawings. . . ."

I went through the bundle. She sure was right. They did get worse. Some of the things that came out of those envelopes would have embarrassed a call girl. And the latrine-wall drawings. . . . I shook my head and bundled the whole mess up.

"Mrs. Rose," I said, "you are obviously the victim of a fairly common variety of crank, a sex pervert, but probably not a dangerous one. Frankly, I'd suggest that you contact either the police or the postal authorities. Naturally, we don't want to turn down business, but they have the facilities to get to the bottom of something like this much faster than a private agency — and at less expense to you."

She looked even more frightened and nervous. "I don't want the police mixed up in this. That's why I've called you, Mr. Scotch. If I called the police, then my husband would have to know all about it, and —"

I raised an eyebrow. "He doesn't know?"

"Of course not, and it will be your business to keep him from find out. I want you to quietly investigate and find out who's sending me all that horrible, nasty stuff and make them quit."

"If you'll pardon this rather personal question, Mrs. Rose, what difference would it make if your husband knew? You surely can't help it if some crank sends stuff like this to you. You're an innocent victim."

Nervously, she pried bits of nail polish off one finger with the thumb nail of her other hand. "Well, I don't want him to find out, that's all. He's very staid and proper. He might not understand. He might get some silly notion that it's an old acquaintance of mine sending that stuff. Or worse, that I'm carrying on with whoever is sending it. You just don't know him. . . ." She made a hopeless gesture with her hand which was supposed to explain everything.

I thought for a moment. "Well, we could try and track down the sender for you. It would be a little hard, not having the help of the postal department, but —"

"Please try and find out for me," she implored. Her green eyes were wide open, pleading. "It's getting so I can't sleep or anything, worrying about it. I'm frightened that one day Martin, that's my husband, will be home when the mail arrives and get one of those letters before I can throw them away. . . ."

I nodded. We got the business of the fee straightened out and she dug a crumpled wad of bills out of a handbag to pay for the first few days' work.

"Now then," I said, "maybe you can give me some leads to go on. The sender is probably somebody who knows you, or has known you in the past." I thought for a minute. "How long have you been married, Mrs. Rose?"

"Six months."

"Hmm. Well, there's the possibility it could be some man you used to know." I didn't say it out loud, but the way she was stacked, I thought she could easily have driven some poor boob sex-nutty. Sore because she had married Rose, maybe he was doing this to annoy her. "Could you give me a list of the men you have known, say in the last couple of years? That will give us something to start on. Also, we'll post a man here in the neighborhood to keep a watch on this building. It's very likely that the guy is hanging around to get a look at you now and then."

Reluctantly, she wrote out a list of names. "Whatever you do, keep these names confidential." She gave me a wise smile. "Husbands don't need to know about the men their wives were acquainted with before they were married, do they?" She gave me the list and shook hands with me. "I feel better already," she said.

Her hand cuddled inside mine for a moment, gave it an intimate squeeze, and she saw me to the door.

May 11

Called on one of the names on the list Evelyn Rose gave me. Guy named Joe McClosky. Ex-prizefighter. Tending bar in a little joint down on Wilson Street now.

I was surprised that a woman of her class would have known a lug like McClosky.

Our conversation ran something like this:

"You Joe McClosky?"

"Yeah. What'll you have, Mister?"

"Bourbon and plain water. You know a lady named Evelyn Rose?"

"Who?"

"Evelyn Rose."

"Here's your bourbon and plain water. Evelyn Rose? Naw. I don't know no dame by that name."

"Red head. Green eyes. Beautiful. Stacked like— "

"Oh, wait a minute. You don't mean Evelyn Janisick, do you? That little red-head that came to town a couple years ago? Was hoofin' over at Steinman's burlesque house?"

"No, that couldn't be her. This is a lady I'm talking about. You know, class. Big shot."

"You kiddin'? If she was that kind of dame what would I be doin' knowin' her?"

I had to admit he had something there.

I went over to the burlesque theater he was talking about. In a back office, I found the owner, Steinman, a bald-headed man with a harrassed face.

"My name is Nick Scotch. Private investigator. Here's my papers."

"Yeah?" The man took a frayed cigar out of his mouth and looked more worried. "What's wrong now?"

"You know a lady named Mrs. Evelyn Rose?"

"I don't know. I don't think so."

I sure had been dumb not to ask Evelyn what her maiden name had been. I went through the description routine again and a light dawned in the man's eyes.

"Well I'll be damned. You mean Evelyn Janisick. Sure, I remember now. It was a guy named Rose she married. . . ."

"Well, you knew her, then."

He looked at me, his small blue eyes amused. "Knew her? Hell, I was married to her."

I sat down and lit a cigarette. Sometimes I think I'm a hell of a judge of character.

"What's she into now?"

"Not a thing. She's been getting things in the mail. Obscene letters. She's hired me to find out who's sending them."

It took a while for the whole thing to sink in. Then Steinman roared. "That's the funniest thing I ever heard."

"It isn't funny to her, mister."

Then I leaned over the desk. "I think maybe it's somebody she used to know who's sending that stuff. I don't know who yet, but I'm just making the rounds to give a warning. If it's you, buster, stop. We're going to find out who's doing it and when we do things are going to get hot for the guy we find."

I had hold of the front of his shirt and gave it a shake for emphasis. His face turned the color of putty and he started swearing.

"That lousy tramp!" he screamed. "She sent you around to strong-arm me, huh? Tell her to go to hell for me. Tell her I don't even remember she's alive! Maybe you should go talk to Joe Wilson, the bookie. He's the guy she was playing around with when she was supposed to be married to me. He's still nuts about her. Ask anybody in this part of town!"

I went out looking for Joe Wilson.

May 12

Spent most of the day checking on old acquaintances of Evelyn's. Threatened each one of them. I figured if one of them was sending the stuff, a threat would be enough to stop them. Not many guys want to chance an argument with Uncle Sam about his mail.

May 14

Met Evelyn in a cocktail bar this afternoon to report on our progress.

She was in the booth when I got there, looking like an Irishman's vision in a Shamrock green suit. She slid over to let me in beside her. When she did, the tight skirt moved above her knees. She didn't bother to put it down.

"Hello, Nick," she said, and put her hand inside mine. "Any luck yet?"

I couldn't take my eyes off her. Neither could I forget that our relationship was on a different plane. The last two days had punctured the pedestal I'd dreamed up for her the first time I saw her.

I ordered a martini. "Well," I said, twiddling with the olive, "I guess I know now why you don't want hubby to find out about the letters."

She gave my hand a tiny squeeze. "I knew you'd find out all about me when you talked with the men I told you about." She took her hand away and lifted her martini to her lips with it. Then she looked down at the drink. "Well?"

"Well, what?"

"What do you think about me now?"

I messed with the olive. "Oh. I guess I think you're a pretty smart cookie."

She sighed. "Do you blame a girl for getting all she can out of life?"

I shrugged. "Well, no. And it isn't any of my business, anyway. You hired me to find out who was sending that obscene matter. That's all."

"I know, but I want you to like me, Nick. I want you to understand."

"I like you," I said.

She flashed me a smile. Under the table, her thigh pressed mine warmly. "It was a tough grind for me, Nick. A girl off a farm. I took my breaks where I could get them. I saved a little money out of the burlesque and being married to Max Steinman. I took a cruise. That's where I met Martin Rose.

He thinks I've changed — but a guy like Martin, he'll never be sure. If he found out about the letters —"

"Yeah," I said. "So, you're extra-sensitive about things like these sex letters."

"I guess so," she admitted. "I'm so afraid all the time that my past will catch up with me. Maybe it is my past. Maybe Max or Joe Wilson or McClosky, or one of those guys are sending that stuff to me. Maybe they're planning to blackmail me."

I shrugged.

"Could be. I tried the direct method. I went to each one, intimated that we had proof that they were sending the stuff and if they didn't quit we'd get the postal authorities on their neck. That should shut them up, if they're just doing it for a prank, or out of a twisted sex motive. If it's blackmail they won't scare so easy."

"What should I do now?"

"Wait a few days. See if it stops. If it doesn't, call me."

She was looking at me. "Nick," she said in a soft, throaty voice. Her lips were parted slightly. She closed her eyes slowly. There was no mistaking what she wanted. And our motto is please the customer.

That gal could kiss, believe me. With little trimmings, like a writhe of her body and a moan that really did it up fine. I got out of there quick, then, before *I* started thinking about sending her frustrated love tokens.

May 15

Evelyn got me at the office, more scared than ever. Wouldn't give the particulars over the phone, just said there was a new development and for me to get myself over to her place quick. I did.

She met me at the door. This time she was dressed in another pair of lounging pajamas, of which she seemed to have endless varieties and colors. Her face was pale. The first thing she said was, "I got another one." Then, "Nick, now I'm really scared."

I walked into her living room and she closed the door. She went to a table and got the letter. "Look. . . ." She handed it to me. Her lips were quivering.

I opened the large kraft envelope. Inside was a glossy eight-by-ten photo. I took it out and looked at it. And then I *really* looked at it.

It was Evelyn and I mean all of Evelyn. She was standing in the middle of her bedroom wearing nothing but a thoughtful expression. She didn't disappoint any of the visions I had conjured up that first day I saw her. She was perfect.

"But *how*, Nick?" she asked. "How could anything like that happen?"

I pursed my lips. After a moment's silence, I said, "Look, Evelyn, I'm a big boy now. Maybe you better tell me —"

"No," she said. "I *swear*, Nick. I swear it isn't anything like that.

Well, maybe I have played around a little, but not in my own bedroom, and I certainly wasn't a fool enough to let anybody take a *picture!*"

I didn't get it at first. Then I got it. A little. Maybe. "It isn't a fake," I said. "Somebody really took a picture of you in your bedroom without any clothes on."

"But nobody *could* have, I tell you."

"He was outside your bedroom window when he took it," I explained. "Look. Here in one corner. You can just see a blur. That's a limb from that big oak tree outside your window. The guy crawled up there and snapped it."

She thought about it and shook her head. "No, I don't see how anybody could have. He would have had to have snapped a flash bulb. I would have seen it."

"They snapped a flash bulb all right," I explained, "but you didn't see it. They probably used an infra-red bulb."

She looked at me wide-eyed. "Oh."

"Yes," I said. "Oh. And now I think we've really got something to go on. I'm going to check all the photo shops in town to see if anybody has been buying infra-red equipment lately."

May 16

Pounded pavement. Asked questions. Got a list of leads. Followed up each one. Did some snooping.

May 17

Got my answer.

"Evelyn?" Me, on the phone.

"Yes?" That's her answer. Both frightened and hopeful.

"I've found him. And it's all right."

There was nothing on her end for a long time, then the sound of her pent-up breath coming out.

"It's no blackmail. Has nothing to do with your past. It's a crank, the way we first thought. A crazy, twisted kid."

"Thank goodness," she said. She was crying.

"Now look. The main thing you don't want to happen is for Daddy to find out things and divorce you, right?"

"That's crude, Nick."

"But right?"

"Yes."

"Okay. Then if you want my advice, you'll play this to the hilt. Tell him. But with tears and histronics. Before he finds out on his own hook. You know, put on the outraged pure white maiden routine. Show him some of the letters. Say you've been keeping it from him, suffering in silence because you didn't want to get him upset until you could find out who it was. Now you know and you want him to protect his home with righteous wrath. He'll eat it up."

She giggled a little. "Nick, you're precious. Oh, I'm so relieved!"

"Don't get too relieved until this

is all over. Call the old man home from work now. I'll meet you with some proper authority, namely a cop." I gave her an address.

"That's right across the street!" she gasped.

"I know," I said.

The boy's name was Jimmy Gavatos. He lived in a cheap, hot, three room flat with his invalid mother. We were all there in an hour, sitting around in the living room, waiting for the kid to come home. Mrs. Gavatos, a frail old lady, sat propped on a couch. Her white, blue-veined hands nervously worried a quilt thrown across her wasted legs. "If you'd only tell me what Jimmy's done," she pleaded, her faded blue eyes going from one of us to the other.

Like I say, there are some times I wish I was a house painter.

"Take it easy, lady," I muttered. "We'd rather talk with Jimmy about it first, when he comes home."

I looked over at Evelyn, who was a study in outraged, humiliated, righteous womanhood, at her husband, Martin, who looked red-faced and angry, and at the plain clothes city detective, who looked bored.

Eventually, we heard the front door open. Somebody came in whistling. "Hey, Ma!" Jimmy entered the sitting room and halted in the doorway, the whistle freezing on his lips.

Martin ran toward him with clutching, trembling fingers. "You rotten, filthy-minded little bastard —"

"Easy, Mr. Rose," the city dick said, stepping between them. "We'll handle the kid. C'mon, Jimmy. We're going down to have a little chat."

Old lady Gavatos sat there, sobbing, looking at us bewilderedly. "Jimmy!" she called in a quavering, frightened voice. "Jimmy. . . ."

I was down there while they questioned the kid. It took a long time. He sat in a straightback chair, sweating, crying a little, refusing to admit to anything. But they kept shoving the stuff at him, all in his handwriting. The clerk at the photography supply house came in and identified him. A neighbor of Evelyn's had seen him hanging around her place.

Finally, he caved in.

"All right," he sobbed hoarsely. "I done it. I sent her the stuff. Now you know, leave me alone. Please, leave me alone. . . ."

I looked at the kid. He was, maybe twenty, twenty-two at the most.

"Why?" the city detective probed.

"None of your goddamn bussiness."

"Why?"

"I told you I done it. Ain't that enough?"

"You must have had a reason, Jimmy," the city detective persisted quietly.

"Naw."

"Did you want money out of her?"

He stared at the floor, sullenly. "Look," he mumbled almost incoherently, "I work all week down at the meat packer's. I don't make much dough. It takes all I make to keep up the apartment an' pay the medicine and stuff Ma needs. There ain't ever any left for me to take a girl out. All week I listen to the guys talkin' around where I work, talkin' about some dame they slept with, or how their wives make love. It bothers me, that stuff they talk about, but I can't never do nuthin' about it, because there ain't ever any money left for me to take a dame out . . . you know."

He wiped the back of his sleeve across his eyes. "That Rose dame. Every night, she undresses with the shades up. Her place is right across the street from me and I can see everything. I think she hopes somebody *does* see — that's why she leaves the shades up. I lay there lookin' at her, every night, listen to the guys talk in the daytime. It eats on me, and I can't do nuthin' about it because, like I say, there ain't any dough left for me to take a dame out." He shrugged. "I don't know why I started sendin' her that stuff. It was just somethin' eatin' at me until I had to do it. . . ."

When I walked out of there, Jimmy was still mumbling that way, half to himself.

May 30.

Went to collect a little bonus on the Evelyn Rose case. Or rather, I just stayed home. The bonus came to me. The bonus, in the form of the delectable Mrs. Rose, herself, sat on my lap, sipping martinis with me until the mood was right. Then she stood up, arranging a slow smoldering smile with one corner of her red lips and a tilt of her left eyebrow.

"Let me get comfy, Nick," she breathed huskily, a promise in her eyes. She went into the bedroom.

I stood over by a window, sipping my drink, looking at the city by night, feeling dirty inside. They were taking Jimmy up the river tonight. They'd laid it on him as heavy as they could. Evelyn's hubby had seen to it that they threw the book at the kid. I stood there wondering about the boy's job, if it would wait for him — and what his invalid mother would do in the meantime.

I wished I'd thought about it before I turned the kid over.

There was a sound in the doorway. Evelyn was there, moving toward me with open willingness on her pouting lips. She was wearing exactly as much as she had in that picture Jimmy took of her. I watched her approach, thinking about Jimmy's crime — having to suppress his own life in order to provide for his mother. A heinous crime. Like hell. She'd asked for it — undressing, deliberately, in front of that window. I took my belt off, holding it by the buckle as she got closer.

Her eyes widened, but she couldn't make herself quite believe what I was going to do. Not until I started doing it. Then it was several seconds before the first agonized scream ripped from her twisted mouth.

The Right Hand of Garth

Garth was no man to fool with, and the new gun we had up from Atlanta knew that. He stood in front of Garth's desk respectfully, and he waited for Garth to speak, and I watched the new man and I watched Garth, and I waited.

Finally, Garth cleared his throat and put his fat fingers on the desk top and he asked, "You served time?"

"No," the new guy said.

"How do I know you're any good?"

"You got the word from Petey."

"I don't trust Petey as far as I can throw him," Garth said. "Petey has sent me some schlemozzles in his time. Petey don't always send me good men."

"I'm a good man," the new guy said.

"How do I know?"

The guy was thin, with

Sparrow was a good man with a gun — and a fast worker with the women. But he got a little too efficient with both . . .

BY EVAN HUNTER

beady black eyes and straight brown hair. He shrugged his shoulders now, and said, "Look, you want me, take me. Otherwise, I'm wasting your time, and you're wasting mine."

"When can you start?" Garth wanted to know.

"Right away."

"Right away means next week, or tomorrow, or five minutes from now," Garth said.

"With me, right away means now. This minute." He looked over to where I sat in the easy chair near Garth's desk. "You want this bastard cooled?" he asked, gesturing at me with his head. "I'll do it. Right away means now with me."

Garth grinned, reached out and patted my knee with one of his fat hands. "He wants to know if I want you cooled, Ed," he said. "Dig that, Ed."

I didn't grin. I looked at the new guy, and I said, "What's your name, tough man?"

"Sparrow," he said. "Sparrow Carter."

I laughed abruptly. "Sparrow! That's for the birds, all right."

"Try me," Sparrow said.

"I just had supper," I told him. I still wasn't smiling.

"Okay, Carter," Garth said, waving one of his hands. "You're in."

"Just like that, huh?" I said.

Garth looked at me, and his mouth was thin. "Just like that, Ed. Any objections?"

"It's your organization," I said.

"And don't forget it."

I got up without looking at Garth. I shot Sparrow a look, and then I said, "I'm going out for some fresh air."

"Don't get lost," Garth said.

I didn't answer. I walked past Sparrow and outside, and then down the long flight of steps to the street. Dusk was on the town. It shadowed the hips of the women, gave a purple tinge to their lips. The neon banners threw orange and red to the night, and the night blared back with black. I walked, and I knew where I was going, and my palms were a little moist, and my step was quick.

I walked all the way, because it was better walking. It was slow, and it gave me a lot of time to think of what was ahead, and I liked that. I liked thinking about it. The thinking of it was almost as good as the reality.

I climbed the steps and rang the doorbell, and I heard four chimes inside, like the Good Humor man on a clear day. When the door opened, I stepped inside quickly, and then closed it behind me, bolting it.

"Ed," she said. "You're early. I thought . . ."

"I got fed up," I said. "Up to here." I passed a hand over my throat. "That big bastard makes me vomit."

"What now?"

"He's taken on a new gun. Some crumb from Atlanta. He calls himself Sparrow." I paused and looked at her. "The hell with them,

Marcie," I said. "The hell with them."

I reached for her, and she ducked away, using that goddamn sidewards motion of hers, ducking her head so that her blonde hair spilled over one shoulder, then moving away like a boxer ducking a punch.

"I want to get dressed, baby," she said.

She looked dressed fine to me. She was wearing green silk that covered her body like spilled molten copper. The dress was knifed down the front in an open V that showed most of her breasts. My hands got moist again, and she saw the look that came over my face, and smiled that wicked, teasing smile of hers.

She had slanted eyes, Marcie, slanted and long, like a Chink's eyes, only better. They were green, and they matched the crooked smile on her mouth, and the small pulse beating in her throat.

"I'll be back," she said.

She walked across the room, and I watched the swing of her hips, and the tightening of her calves. I watched her until she closed the door on my gaze. Then I sat down and lighted a cigarette, and I thought of Garth and the new character, Sparrow. A nice pair. Fat and Skinny. *Fat and Skinny ran a race, all around the pillow case . . .*

I smoked the cigarette down to a butt, and then I heard her call, "Ed. Eddie."

I got up and walked to the closed door. "Yeah, baby?"

"Come in, Eddie. I want you to help me."

I opened the door, and she was standing with her back to me, and the long mirror on the wall showed me her front. Her legs were long and curved, and the black lace made them seem longer. She was reaching behind her for a clasp, and the narrow black strap cut into the firm flesh of her back.

"Here," she said. "Do me."

I walked over to her, and my hands were trembling when I took the silk strap. I started to clasp it for her, and my knuckles touched the cool flesh of her back, and I dropped the strap. I reached around her with my hands cupped, and she moved back against me and threw her head back and I kissed the side of her neck, and the hollow under her shoulder bone. She turned in my arms, and she lifted her mouth, and her lips were wide and soft and wet and warm.

"Eddie," she said, "Eddie, baby. We . . . we got to . . . not now, Eddie. Garth . . ."

"The hell with Garth," I said viciously. I clamped my mouth onto hers, and she went limp in my arms, and the black silk and lace dropped to the floor at my feet.

"Eddie, no . . ."

"You knew this would happen," I said. "When you called me in . . ."

"I knew," she whispered. "I knew, I knew."

We spent the night at a joint

called *The Bar*. Garth sat on one side of the table, with Marcie's hand clamped in his big fist. She was wearing a black strapless, and from where I was sitting only a little bit of the dress showed above the table top, and the rest was all Marcie. I wet my lips, and kept my eyes off her. Sparrow sat next to me, looking more like a snake than a bird. When the showgirls came out, he undressed every one of them with his eyes, and when they were gone, he started doing the same to Marcie.

Garth was in his cups. He never could drink good, and he was really pouring them down his fat mouth tonight. He didn't seem to notice the way Sparrow was ogling Marcie, but I noticed, and I didn't like it, and I added one more name to my personal spit list.

Along about midnight, Garth looked at his watch and said, "Okay, Sparrow. Okay, now. Okay, you better get started."

Sparrow looked at his own watch, lifting his skinny wrist. Then he nodded and stood up, and from where he was standing he could probably look down to Marcie's navel, and he did.

"I'll be back," he said.

Garth nodded, and Sparrow took off, and I watched him go and then asked, "What's up?"

"Greene," Garth said.

"What about Greene?"

"He's got a appointment." Garth smiled. "In Samarra." He smiled again. "You know what that means, Ed?"

"No," I said.

"That's 'cause you're a stupid bastard," Garth told me. "Marcie, you know what that means, don't you?"

"No," Marcie said.

"Appointment in Samarra. Don't any of you read books?"

"What's gonna happen to Greene?" I asked.

"You guess. You guess what Sparrow's gonna do to him. You guess what he's gonna do to that filthy bastard."

"I'm not good at guessing. You tell me."

"You'll read it in the papers," Garth said. "Greene's getting a little too ambitious, Ed. You might keep that in mind."

"Why?"

"You just might, that's all." He squeezed Marcie's hand and then said, "Ed, why the hell don't you go home? Marcie and me got business, eh, Marcie?" When she didn't answer he said, "Marcie?"

Marcie nodded. "If you say."

"I say. Come on, let's all get the hell out of here. You go home, Ed, and me and Marcie'll have our business."

"What about Sparrow? He said he'd be back."

"He's a big boy now," Garth said. "He'll find his way home. Come on, let's cut out."

We cut out, and when I got the

newspapers the next morning, it was all over page four. Greene had been found dead in an alley in the Village. Someone had planted four .45 caliber slugs in his belly, and then stuck the muzzle in his mouth and blown the top of his head off for good measure. Someone.

The newspapers didn't say that the someone was Sparrow.

The rumble had it, though. The rumble spread goddamn fast, and all the boys began talking him up. Sparrow this and Sparrow that until it was coming out of my ears. I didn't say anything to Garth because I didn't want him to think it bothered me. It bothered me a hell of a lot, though.

He was all the time talking about what a good boy Sparrow was, and how Petey had really come through with a winner for a change. He told me he wished he had a dozen like Sparrow, and he told me that with a straight face, like he really believed it. I let it ride. I let it ride because I was still seeing Marcie, and every time her flesh was in my hands, I thought of Garth and of how I was fooling the fat bastard.

When the carry away job came up, Garth told me about it first.

"They got this safe laying in the loft," he said, "and all they got is a half-blind watchman on it. We put him away, grab the safe, and open it in our own good time."

"That ain't so easy," I said. "A carry away . . ."

"There's an elevator leading to the loft," Garth said. "We bring a dolly up with us, lay out the old man, and then wheel the safe to the elevator. When we get down, we wheel it down the ramp and into the trunk of the car. It's like taking candy, Ed."

"Who'll make the caper?"

"You and Sparrow."

"Why him?"

"Why not? You two'll hit the safe. I'll send Davie along to drive. That should be enough on something as simple as this."

"Sure. But why Sparrow?"

"He's good with a gun."

"Anybody's good with a gun. All you need is a forefinger to be good with a gun."

"Sparrow's very good."

"Maybe he's too good."

"How do you mean?"

"Blowing off Greene's skull. That wasn't necessary."

Garth smiled. "You see, Ed, that's where we're different. I thought it was a nice touch." He paused. "We'll hit the loft tomorrow night. You, Davie, and Sparrow."

"And you?"

"I'll wait for you." He grinned. "At Marcie's place."

"I figured," I said. "Okay. Tomorrow night."

We made it the next night. It was an easy caper, and we didn't expect any trouble. We drove right up to the loft, and I cracked the lock on the outside gate and then we walked up the ramp and jimmied one of the windows. Davie kept the engine running, with his lights out, and the black car blended right in with the shadows between the buildings. We already had the trunk up, and the planks leading from the ground to the trunk were in place.

I carried the dolly, and I went through the window first, with Sparrow behind me. We walked up stairs, and then pussyfooted it when we heard the watchman making his rounds.

"I'll take him," Sparrow said.

I nodded, and we heard the watchman coming closer, whistling. We waited until he walked by, and then Sparrow reached out and wrapped one hand around his throat, pulling him back. He brought up his .45 and clubbed it down on the top of the old man's skull. I knew he'd hit him hard enough to fell him the first time, but he kept clubbing the old man, bringing the .45 up and down like a piston, finally letting the poor bastard fall to the floor.

"Why'd you hit him so hard?" I whispered. "You want to kill the bastard?"

"He was struggling," Sparrow said.

"My ass was struggling."

"Come on, let's hit the safe."

We found the safe just where Garth said it would be. We tilted the sonovabitch until we got one end on the dolly, and then it was clear sailing. We wheeled it to the elevators, took a car down, and then opened the front doors wide. We rolled the dolly and safe down the ramp and right to the back of the car. Davie got out then, and we all shoved and got the safe rolled up into the trunk. We closed the trunk, threw the dolly in the back seat, climbed in, and drove away.

We were two blocks from the loft when we spotted the patrol car.

"Play it cool," I said. "We're not known here. We're three guys out for a drive, you follow? If they make a move for the trunk, then we blast. But cool otherwise, understand?"

"Who died and left you boss?" Sparrow asked.

"Shut up, you bastard," I said. "We got enough problems right now."

The patrol car swung in a wide arc when we passed it, and then started after us, driving slowly.

"Keep it under 35," I told Davie. "Those guys ain't suspicious. They're just killing time."

Davie nodded and kept driving slowly, and the patrol car kept behind us for a little while, then swung out and moved up.

"They're coming," Davie said.

"All right, just keep cool."

The cops pulled alongside, and I got to admit Davie was the coolest. He looked out the window on his side, and smiled, and the cop smiled back and was lifting his hand to wave when Sparrow cut loose.

The .45 went off right near my

head, and I heard the explosions, five in a row, fast, and I smelled the stench of cordite. And then the patrol car was out of control and swerving over toward the curb.

"Step on it!" Sparrow yelled.

Davie gave it the gun, and Sparrow fired the remaining shots in the clip as the patrol car climbed the curb and slammed into the brick side of a building. Davie really went then, and we cut through that city like a lawnmower, and when we pulled up in front of Marcie's place, there wasn't a soul behind us.

"Why'd you do that?" I said.

"You think those guys were out for a Sunday drive?" Sparrow said. "Man, they were ready to pounce."

"Like the old man in the loft, huh?" I asked.

"Can it, Ed. Just can it. We got away, didn't we?"

"Yeah," I said. "This time."

Well, the rumble really went out that time. That time, they played it up real fine. The way they told it, Sparrow had climbed out of the car and knocked off a whole National Guard unit with a peashooter. Garth was pleased as hell, and the word started getting around that there was a new right hand man, and his name was Sparrow. And a right hand man is nothing to scoff at. Sparrow was the right hand of Garth, and there was talk about cutting him in for a five-five split, talk like that.

I listened to the talk, and it burned me, but I didn't say anything. I was waiting until I could see Marcie again. We'd talk it over then.

After the carry away, Garth wanted a little celebration. He took us on the town, all the boys, and Marcie, of course. One thing you had to say for Garth, he was a big spender. There must have been twenty of us in the club that night, and Garth bought for them all night long. Everybody kept coming over to Sparrow and congratulating him on the cop kill, never mentioning it out loud just like that, but saying it so he knew what they meant.

Sparrow took it all like a modest hero. He sat there with one of Garth's cigars in his mouth, relaxed next to Marcie with one hand under the table, and the other resting in his lap. Marcie's dress was something, all right, and I think the guys came up more to look down at Marcie than to congratulate Sparrow. But they came up anyway, and each time they bulled him, it burned me up more. I sat there smoking cigarette after cigarette, and getting sorer and sorer.

I finally started to light another butt, and my hands were shaking so much that I dropped the matchbook. I got down on my hands and knees under the table. Sparrow was taking more compliments, and Marcie was starting on her fourth or fifth martini, and I was still sore as hell. I got under the table, and I found the matches, and then I saw Marcie's legs, with her skirt hiked up around her thighs, and the ribbed tops of her stockings tight against her flesh, with the garters taut like springs. I wanted to reach up for her, and then I saw the hand resting on her thigh, resting there tight with the fingers digging into the flesh. I thought it was Garth at first, and then I realized the hand was skinny, like a claw, and I knew it was Sparrow's hand, and I wanted to break it at the wrist and throw it in his face. I got out from under the table, and the party was still going on, with no one even noticing my absence. I looked at Marcie, but she didn't look back at me. Sparrow hunched forward, and his arm went a little deeper under the table, and I saw Marcie's lips part a little in surprise. I thought she was going to cry out at first, but instead she just lifted her drink and took a quiet sip, and when she took the glass from her lips, her mouth was still open, and her head was tilted back a little, with the blonde hair falling over her shoulders, and there was a sort of glazed look in her eyes that didn't come from martinis.

I looked at her, and she took a deep breath, and her breasts bunched against the low front of her dress and Sparrow looked at her sideways. Garth was talking it up with the boys; he didn't notice anything.

But Sparrow didn't take his hand from under that table all night long, and Marcie just sat there like a hypnotized chicken, and that was the night Sparrow made his appointment, in Samarra like Garth would say.

Maybe Garth didn't notice anything that night, but the rest of the boys weren't blind, and they saw everything that went on. I figured that was in my favor, and when I laid my plan, I took that into account. I began talking it up a little, letting the rumble sneak out. I began saying how Sparrow was really getting to be the right hand, and maybe the left hand, and maybe a couple of other things, too. I let that out quiet-like, just so the rumble would get started, you know. Just so the guys would think Sparrow was muscling in where he should have stood in bed.

I called Marcie a couple of times, and each time she told me she was going shopping, or to the beauty parlor, or something like that.

I knew she was lying, of course, and that burned me more. I couldn't figure how a skinny runt like Sparrow rated with somebody like Marcie, and especially after what had gone between us. I kept thinking, maybe she's reading the cards. Maybe she figures I'm washed up, and when Garth hands in his holster, it'll be Sparrow who fronts the boys.

I kept thinking that, and even that made me sore. Marcie had been around for a long time now. All the boys knew her and liked her, and all the boys knew about her and me, too. Marcie knew who was top man before Sparrow came along, and all the boys knew *that*, too. If anything ever happened to Garth, it was me who'd take over, and I'd take over in every department, and there'd be no more sneaking up to Marcie's joint, no more looking over my shoulder for Garth to catch me with my hand on her hip.

But all that was before Sparrow, and when the boys saw what was going on between him and Marcie, they began to look at me a little differently. I helped them because that was just what I wanted. I wanted them to think I was out in the cold. I wanted them to think Sparrow was edging in, and I wanted them to think he was edging in most of all on Marcie.

There can only be one right hand. But if the head is blown off, and the right hand is cut off —then the left hand takes over. I was happy to be the left hand. That was the way I wanted it. And so, where I was happy with my position, I was sore because Marcie couldn't understand what I was trying to swing.

I'd sit up at night and think of her in Sparrow's arms, with his skinny hands crawling over her flesh like white spiders. I'd think of that, and it would burn me up because Marcie was being stupid. She was putting her money on the wrong horse, and when the race was over — well, that was where I consoled myself. When the race was over, when Garth and Sparrow both lost out, I'd forgive Marcie. I'd be big about it. I'd say hell, a girl can make a mistake, and you can't blame anyone for picking a loser. Everybody's got to make his own way in this goddamn world. I'd forgive her, and then I'd spend the rest of my life as the big cheese, with Marcie's flesh mine whenever I wanted it, with no sneaking around. And my forgiving her would really put her in line. A woman doesn't like to be wrong, and when she's wrong in something as big as this was, she never steps out of line again.

That's why I was pleased and sore all at the same time, but mostly pleased because things were running along just the way I wanted them.

Sparrow got more and more confident. Garth gave him two or three more torpedo jobs, and he polished them off very efficiently and expertly, even though I felt he decorated the jobs a little. That was the way he was in everything. He overdressed, and he overkilled.

With each job, he seemed to get bolder with Marcie. After the carry away, he had held Marcie's thigh under the table, and he was very careful. When he knocked off Rabinowitz on the East Side, he danced with Marcie all night long, and only a blind man could miss seeing where he held her. When Torqui the Bum got refrigerated, Sparrow took a long walk with Marcie, leaving the party and coming back with his face all stained with lipstick.

I helped him the next time. I'd been talking it up all this while, and whereas I knew Garth had no inkling at all of what was going on, I made to the boys like he did. I told them he was sore, and that he was waiting, just waiting for Sparrow to really step out of line. The boys took me at face value because I was, after all, the guy who'd been dumped out of bed. They figured I knew, and I let them think that, and the night Marty Bishop was rubbed, I helped Sparrow.

We were in this dump, I forget the name, and things were running along just like always. I kept watching Sparrow and Marcie, the way his hands touched her whenever he thought Garth wasn't watching. He didn't care about anyone else, just Garth. Garth, as usual, was drinking like a fish, and Marcie just sat there with the strange half-smile on her face, letting Sparrow do whatever he wanted to do. She was drinking pretty heavily, and along about midnight she began looking a little green around the gills.

I nudged Garth and said, "Marcie's stoned."

Garth was stoned himself, so he looked up and nodded and then went back to his scotch. Marcie kept drinking, and then she sort of rolled sideways and Sparrow caught her under the armpits, and I watched the quick way his hands worked as he pretended to help her.

"Garth," I said, "Marcie's ready for bed."

Garth threw off some more scotch. "Marcie's always ready for bed," he said bitterly.

"I'll tell Sparrow to take her home, Garth," I said. "Okay?"

"Why? She sick?"

"She's going to be. Damned soon. I'll tell Sparrow to take her home."

Garth nodded, and I don't think he knew what the hell I was talking about. "All right. Go ahead. Okay."

I gave the word to Sparrow, and he looked at me with those small black eyes of his, and then smiled, and I knew he was thinking he'd pulled a shrewdie on all of us. He helped Marcie to her feet, with those damned white-spider hands of his working all the time, over her hips, her thighs, touching the low front of her dress. He led her out of this dump, I forget the name, and the party went on without them, just as if they'd never been there. I gave them time to get home, and then I gave them time to get friendly, and then I started on Garth.

"Funny about Marcie," I said.

Garth looked up and said nothing. He was studying my face, trying to focus the features.

"She was feeling all right," I said, "and all of a sudden, she don't look so good."

"Happens that way," Garth said.

"Sure. Especially when Sparrow's around so eager to get her home."

I let that penetrate. Garth looked into the open circle of his scotch glass, and I thought for a minute he didn't hear me. Then he lifted his head in a series of jerky motions, and said, "What?" He said it as if I'd asked him for the time or something and he hadn't heard me too well.

"Nothing," I said.

"No, what'd you say?"

"Nothing. Just about Sparrow, that's all."

"What about Sparrow?"

"Him and Marcie. It's probably my imagination."

Garth blinked his eyes and put down his glass, and I knew I was finally reaching him.

"What d'you mean, him and Marcie? What's that supposed to mean?"

"Nothing, Garth."

"Don't 'nothing' me, you bastard. What are you driving at?"

"I mean it, Garth. Nothing. So he took her home, so what? What the hell does that mean?"

"She was sick. You said so yourself," Garth said, and I wondered how drunk he really was.

"Well, she looked sick," I said. "Until . . . never mind."

"Until what?"

"Until, well, until she walked out of here with him. She looked okay then. Look, Garth, forget about it, will you? It's probably nothing."

"You trying to say . . ." He stopped talking, as if he himself had just realized what I was trying to say. He stroked his fat lips, and he began sweating, and he sat there thinking for a long time. Then he got up, and he said, "You heeled?"

"Sure," I said.

"Come on, Ed. And God help you if you're wrong."

All the boys saw us go, and they all saw the look on Garth's face, so they knew just where we were heading. I smiled to myself because this was going to be fine, and in the morning the boys would be taking their orders from me. We grabbed a cab outside, and we went straight to Marcie's place. We took the elevator up, and Garth kept clenching and unclenching his hands all the way up. I knew he didn't carry a gun any more because he had plenty of boys to do the carrying for him. That made things even better. I'd only have one to worry about. I thought of the setup, and how sweet it was, and I was laughing fit to bust inside, even though I wore a deadpan outside. We got out of the elevator and walked down the hall, and Garth took out his key and twisted it in the lock of Marcie's door. The lights were out in the living room, just like I'd figured, and we could see a narrow shaft of yellow spilling from under the closed bedroom door. Garth looked at me, and he nodded grimly, and I took the .38 out of my shoulder holster and threw off the safety.

We walked across the thick rug to the bedroom, and I was thinking, I'll be walking on this rug long after you're gone, you fat bastard.

Garth stopped outside the bedroom door for just a second. Then he grabbed the knob and threw it open, and I was right beside him, with the gun pointed right at where I knew the bed would be.

They were framed there like some goddamn cheap movie you see in the penny arcades. Marcie, with her blonde hair spilling over her naked shoulders; Sparrow with his spider-white hands crawling over her body.

Marcie jumped off the bed when we came in, and Sparrow reached under the pillow for his .45. Garth yelled, "You lousy sonovabitch!" and that was when I cut loose with the .38. I fired four shots, blasting the hell out of Sparrow's face.

Garth stood trembling in the doorway of the room, his big body moving like a dish of angry jello. I walked over to the bed, and because Sparrow liked to be fancy, I put the muzzle of the .38 against his heart, and I gave him one more blast for good luck. Then I reached under the pillow for him, picking up the .45.

I swung the gun around at Garth, and when he saw it, he looked as if he didn't believe it. "What is this?" he asked. "What is this, Ed?"

"It's a double kill," I said. "Two crazy bastards after the same broad. You shoot Sparrow with the .38, and Sparrow kills you with the .45. All very simple, Garth."

"What do you mean? What the hell . . ."

I opened up with the .45, and it was a really beautiful thing to see. The holes appeared around Garth's middle, and he brushed at them like a guy does trying to shake beetles loose. The holes traveled up his front, dotting his chest, and then I put the last two shots in his face, and he fell forward like a mountain, hitting the rug and not moving again. Marcie was leaning against the dresser, trying to hold her flimsy nightgown to her. She smiled at me, and I smiled back, and she said, "That was very smart, Ed."

I went about my business, waiting for her to apologize. I wrapped Sparrow's hand around the .45, and I put his finger inside the trigger guard and around the trigger. Then I put the .38 into Garth's fist, and it looked just the way I wanted it to. Two guys blasting at each other in a jealous rage.

"Let's get out of here," I said to Marcie.

"Sure," she said. "I've got to dress, Ed."

She turned and opened the drawer behind her, and the nightgown tightened across her back, and her flesh shone like dull ivory beneath it. I watched her, and my palms began to sweat again, and when she turned, I looked up at her face quickly.

I saw the look in her eyes first. And then the wide grin on her mouth. I felt a sick panic. It hit me all at once, and I knew Sparrow hadn't been the right hand, and neither had I. There'd been another inheritor all along, another person who'd planned on taking control.

There was the real right hand of Garth, and it held a pearl-handled .22, and bright red fingernails curled around the gleaming grip.

"Marcie . . ." I said.

"It worked fine, Ed," she said, almost purring, taking a step closer, still smiling widely. "Just the way I wanted it to. You were a very good boy, Ed. You figured very smart."

"Marcie, Jesus . . ."

But some of Sparrow must have rubbed off on her, and when she squeezed the trigger, there was a crazy kill light in her eyes, and I thought *Christ, what a bitch she'll be to work for.*

And then the slug took me between the eyes.

I didn't see her when she took the .45 from Sparrow's hand and replaced it with the .22.

Nor did I feel anything when she pressed the .45 tight into my own hand.

My right hand.

CRIME CAVALCADE

BY VINCENT H. GADDIS

Cheating Cops

A civil service examination for the posts of sergeant and lieutenant in the Philadelphia, Pa., police department was cancelled recently. Somebody stole the test questions. The city's Personnel Director Frank J. Escobedo said a clerk in the county commissioner's office had been caught selling answers to the examination questions to some of the 600 patrolmen and sergeants who were to have taken the tests.

Muscle Man

In Hartford, Conn., officers noticed that Donald R. Marsan, 17, was sweating excessively as they questioned him in connection with a bad check case. At first they suspected his sense of guilt made him uncomfortably warm, then they wondered. Finally, they asked him to remove his sweater. Marsan proceeded to peel off 17 sweaters. He explained that he wore the extra garments to make him look like a prize fighter.

Strip Shoplifters

Two women acquired new dresses at a store in Manhasset, N. Y., by simply putting on the dresses and walking out, police reported recently. Wearing only slips under their overcoats, the pair asked to try on several dresses. A few minutes later they returned from the dressing room and laid down the garments, saying they had decided not to purchase any of them. A clerk with a sharp memory, however, became suspicious when one of the dresses she recalled giving the women was not returned. She notified a house detective and police, who caught the pair a few blocks away.

Twenty Story Escape

A murder suspect has shattered the reputation of the "escape-proof" jail at Miami, Fla., located on the 20th floor of a skyscraper. The suspect disappeared, but was recaptured on the streets several hours later. He explained that he found a garden hose, fastened one end of it to a pipe and slid down to the 18th floor, entered a window, then waited for an elevator which carried him to freedom.

Hits Jackpot

Rep. Robert O. Cunningham, the Oklahoma State Legislature's anti-crime crusader, accompanied Oklahoma City police on a vice raid. He placed a nickel in the slot of a machine which looked suspiciously like an illegal gambling device. Out came 148 nickels. A reporter asked the legislator if he intended to keep the money. "Certainly," he replied. "It was my nickel!"

One Never Knows

Police at Dayton, O., were ordered to search for Robert Rickle following a report from nearby Hamilton that he was wanted there for auto theft and forgery. At his home the officers got a clue. They found their man at police headquarters. He had just scored the highest grade among a group of applicants for appointments to the force.

Twin Bullets

One of the most remarkable freak occurrences in the history of firearms happened several years ago in a Cleveland, O., apartment. A young bride was found lying across a bed, shot to death. Police found the gun behind a trunk along the wall ten feet from the bed. An autopsy disclosed that two bullets had penetrated the victim's heart. The husband claimed that his wife had committed suicide following a quarrel that had been overheard by neighbors. Since officers were certain that no one could shoot himself twice and then conceal the gun, they arrested the husband on a murder charge.

One of the detectives, however, was puzzled by the fact that the bullets had peculiar shapes, and he found that there was only one bullet hole in the body. After consulting experts, he discovered that the first bullet had apparently been jammed in the barrel for some time. When the weapon was fired in the apartment, the second bullet struck the first, and both passed through the barrel and penetrated the woman's body. As a result, the terrific recoil kicked the gun from the victim's hand to a wall, where it fell behind the trunk.

The husband was released.

Too Much Promotion

Vandals cut the halyards of seven flagpoles in Lancaster, Pa., and each time it meant another job for Lyle Demora, a steeplejack. Finally police caught two men in the act. They were charged with malicious destruction of property after they admitted they were Demora's employees, while the steeplejack was placed under arrest as an accessory.

Thread of Evidence

Police in Oklahoma City were called to the home of Mrs. Nora McPhail one night after she arrived home and found that a burglar had entered through a window and taken a radio and a portable sewing machine.

The officers noticed that a thread had dropped from the sewing machine and left a trail through the window and away from the building. They followed the thread and found a man sound asleep in a nearby weed patch, the missing radio and sewing machine at his side.

Missing Major

The case of Major Robert L. Clark seems destined to join that of Judge Crater in the classic annals of mysterious disappearances. Major Clark, 33, a member of the headquarters staff of the Southeastern Defense Command during World War II, was last seen by fellow officers as he left Raleigh, N. C., in his private car for Fort Bragg on March 17, 1944. Seventy-two hours later he was listed AWOL and an intensive search that lasted for weeks was launched by local and state police, the FBI, and military authorities.

Seven months later a hunter found his car in a woods near Montrose, N. C., where it had been carefully concealed under vines, pinebrush and leaves. In the car were three handbags containing his clothing and other personal possessions, including his gun. An empty woman's handbag was found near the car. Another futile search was made in the area.

Authorities found no evidence of violence and no reason why Clark would have engineered his own disappearance. His bank accounts were intact, he enjoyed his work and he had been having no difficulties in his personal life.

Many of Clark's friends, who said he had the habit of picking up hitchhikers, believe he was murdered. If so, his body has never been found.

Wrong Day

David Graham, alcohol tax agent, found six cases of bootleg whiskey under the pulpit of the Hadkin Grove Baptist church near Salisbury, N. C. He arrested a member of the congregation as a suspect. When newspaper reporters asked Graham why he considered this particular man as a suspect, the agent replied: "He showed up at church today. And it's not Sunday."

Stomach Solution

Police in Detroit have discovered that the way to nab youthful burglars is through their stomachs. Two detectives trailed a 14-year-old boy suspect and watched him break into a candy store and drink three milk-shakes. When he slipped out with more milk-shakes in containers, they followed him to the home of a chum where three other boys were waiting. Questioning of the boys solved 44 burglaries in the neighborhood.

Out Again, In Again

Two prisoners in the Burlington, Vt., jail recently escaped, robbed an express company safe of $400, and then broke back into jail. Sheriff Dewey Perry identified the prisoners as Fred Hamelin, 27, and Clyde A. Hamblin, 26. He said the men pried some bricks loose from the basement of the jail, crossed the yard and walked three blocks down the street. There they entered Gay's Express office, battered open the safe, then returned and re-entered the jail, replacing the bricks.

The sheriff said the break might have gone unnoticed if the prisoners hadn't begun acting "sort of strange." A search of the cells revealed the money hidden in the bedding of the two men.

Problem of the Pipe

Officials of an alcohol plant in Lille, France, worried over constant "evaporation" of high grade alcohol from a large vat, emptied the vat recently for the first time in years. At the bottom they found an outlet which shouldn't have been there.

Police dug under the vat around the outlet pipe and found a six foot high tunnel, leading 200 yards to a garage owned by a neighbor, Edward Welcome. In the garage was a 200 gallon vat of alcohol.

The tunnel was equipped with electric lights, as well as a miniature railway complete with tank cars and a small engine that ran on — you guessed it — alcohol. Welcome admitted that he had been stealing alcohol over a 13-year period and selling it in nearby Belgium where prices were higher.

Artistic Anger

Intruders who broke into the Williams Paint Store in South Bend, Ind. were unsuccessful in their effort to open the office safe. They vented their frustration on the store's stock, dumping over a hundred gallons of paint of various colors over the floor, fixtures and office furniture. Damage was estimated at over $1000.

Strip Tease

When Rosario Jose Diaz, a young pickpocket, snatched a wallet from the pocket of a fellow street car passenger in Buenos Aires, his victim turned and seized him. Diaz escaped by wriggling out of his coat. Then the conductor grabbed him. After a brief struggle Diaz freed himself again and the conductor was left holding his shirt and suspenders. Diaz jumped off the car and started to run, holding his pants with his hands. Then his rapidly moving legs jerked the pants from his hand, and he tripped and fell. That was how police caught him.

Double Check

Detectives in Memphis, Tenn., are looking for the person who cashed a check in a department store drawn on the "East Bank of the Mississippi." And in Indianapolis, Ind., the man who cashed a fraudulent check in a grocery store recently is still at large. The check was signed "U. R. Stuck."

Loot Hangs High

The burglary business in Butte, Mont., is looking up. Loot taken from a tavern included a hundred one dollar bills on which customers had written their names.

The bills had been tacked to the ceiling.

Living Loot

The thieves who broke into the Hollywood, Calif., Aquarium recently apparently intended to start a jungle. The loot included a 6-foot water boa, an 8-foot indigo snake, two 5-foot boa constrictors and a rare Siamese gekko lizard. Sylvester C. Lloyd, owner of the aquarium, said the lizard should be easy to recognize because it has big feet. In southeast Asia, he explained, the gekko is kept in houses to eat the roaches, and runs around all night making a noise that sounds like "gekko."

Bullet Proof

Thirty-two years ago Donato DiGiovanni, 68, of Torrington, Conn., was shot by a holdup man. Doctors removed the slug from his chest several weeks ago while performing a gall bladder operation.

Candidate for Oblivion

Members of the Theft Detecting Society at Woodstock, Conn., agree that they receive little encouragement these days. Believed to be the oldest society of its kind in the nation, its 160th annual meeting was held recently. The organization was founded in Colonial times to catch horse thieves.

Back to the Scene

A visitor to Milwaukee, Wis., admitted he held up a restaurant, boarded a bus, got confused and returned to the scene of his crime. Police were waiting when Kenneth Carlisle, of Vassar, Mich., got off the bus in front of the restaurant and was recognized by his victim. Carlisle told officers he wandered around Milwaukee after robbing a waitress of $140, then got on a bus and lost his sense of direction. "Guess I just had bad luck," Carlisle said.

Number One Crime

According to the FBI, auto theft is the nation's number one crime against property. An estimated 90,000 automobiles — an average of one car every seven minutes — were stolen last year. The cars were valued at $200,000,000.

Ninety percent of the thefts, federal agents said, were the fault of the owners. A survey made in a large eastern city two years ago revealed that 11 percent of the stolen cars had been left with their keys in the ignition switch. Seventeen percent had been left with the doors unlocked, enabling a thief to lift the hood and start the car without a key. One percent of the owners had conveniently placed the keys behind the sun visor.

Easy Does It

In Frankfort, Ind., arresting Leo Sipes was the easiest job police ever had. Sipes slipped in a back door at headquarters and took the first bed he saw. It happened to be in a cell. Officers found him there asleep and quietly closed and locked the door. He appeared in city court next morning charged with public intoxication.

You Can't Win

Officers in Kalamazoo, Mich., spent several hours recently dragging the river for Ura Johnson, who was believed to have drowned. However he finally showed up — alive.

Instead of thanking the cops for their efforts, Johnson bawled them out for describing him in newspaper reports as "shabbily dressed."

Six Stories Up

CHIEF OF POLICE Charlie Shannon leaned a little further out the window of room 607 and said, "Paul . . . Paul, listen to reason."

The boy on the narrow, slanting ledge of the City Hall building didn't look at Shannon. He was staring down at the crowd that had gathered six stories below to watch and wait. It was almost four o'clock now, and he had been out on the ledge since shortly after two.

"Paul . . ." Shannon said.

"Let me alone," the boy said. "I'm not coming in." He glanced at Shannon, and then away again. The eyes in the pinched, sweat-sheened face were sick with fear. "I tell you I didn't kill him!"

"No," Shannon said. "Of course you didn't. We all know that, Paul."

"He was a good guy," Paul said. "He was real good to me. I —" His voice broke.

The kid stood out on the ledge, ready to jump — because they'd accused him of murder. And at least one man wanted the kid to jump . . .

BY

RAYMOND J. DYER

"You've got nothing to fear," Shannon said. "I give you my word on that. Now, why don't you let the firemen put the ladder up? You can climb down, and we'll talk it over."

"No," Paul said. "If they try to put a ladder up, or spread a net out down there, I'm going to jump."

"Paul, listen to reason. Your father's on his way here now. He —"

"Get away from me!" Paul said. "If you don't leave me alone, I'm going to jump right now!"

Shannon looked down at the street, at the policemen working to keep the crowd back from the place where Paul's body would land. He moistened his lips. They'd never be able to get a ladder up or spread a net, he knew. The kid was crazed with fear; he'd do just what he'd said he would. When he saw the net or ladder, he'd jump.

Behind him someone said, "Chief . . ." and Shannon drew his shoulders back through the window and faced the room. They were all still there; the priest and Detective-Sergeant Bailey and the two uniformed cops.

"Chief," Sergeant Bailey said, "the commissioner just called. He's on his way over." He shook his head. "He's plenty hot, Chief."

"So he's plenty hot," Shannon said. "What the hell can I do about it? Right now, I'm more interested in getting that kid off that ledge."

The priest and one of the uniformed cops went to the window and began to talk to Paul.

"You think he killed Sorrentino, Chief?" Bailey asked.

"Hell no, he didn't kill him," Shannon said. "I talked to him long enough to be sure of that."

"Maybe Sorrentino ain't dead," Bailey said. "Maybe he just wanted to disappear."

"If he's dead, that kid didn't kill him," Shannon said. "He couldn't kill anyone." He looked away from Bailey for a moment. "I know about kids that age. I got a boy fifteen myself, remember?"

"Yeah, Chief, but —"

"This kid's just panicked, that's all," Shannon said. "My Chester would be the same way, if it was him out there." His voice suddenly hardened. "He's just a kid and he's scared to death, and if you had been on the job he wouldn't be out there now."

"Jesus, Chief. All I did was turn my back a second, and he was gone."

"The kid didn't kill him," Shannon said. "We can't let him jump off that ledge, Bailey."

"If we could only get a line on Sorrentino," Bailey was saying when the police commissioner came in.

"What the hell's it all about, Charlie?" the commissioner asked. "What kind of a show are you putting on here, anyway?" He crossed directly to the window, and the priest and uniformed cop stood back to let him look out.

"It seemed hopeless, Commissioner," the priest said. "We've tried everything. The boy —"

The commissioner ignored him. "This is one hell of a fine mess. Who is he, anyway?"

Chief Shannon sat down and the commissioner came up and stood over him.

"His name's Paul Merton," Shannon said. "We had a wire out on him. He worked for a guy named Sorrentino in a restuarant over on Mill Street. Sorrentino and the kid both disappeared about a week ago, just after Sorrentino took a couple thousand out of the bank." He glanced once again at the open window. "The Oglethorpe police picked the kid up driving Sorrentino's car."

"What about this Sorrentino?" the commissioner asked.

"No sign of him."

"The kid killed him?"

Shannon shook his head. "No. And maybe he isn't dead. Anyhow, I hope not."

"The hell you hope not," the commissioner said. "You better start hoping he's dead, and that that kid out there killed him. Otherwise, we're all in the soup." He glared at Shannon. "Where's this brat from?"

"St. Louis," Shannon said. "He ran away from home six months ago. We've wired his father. He's on his way here by plane."

"God," the commissioner said. "With election and appointments coming up, you had to pull something like this."

"He's innocent," Shannon said.

"To hell with that kind of talk. Jim Pealy and his crowd'll crucify you and me and the whole damn department if he gets hold of that innocent talk." He leaned down close to Shannon and dropped his voice to a whisper. "As far as we're concerned, that kid's as guilty as hell. Get me?"

"You're crazy, Tom," Shannon said. "What's he guilty of? Murder? Then where's the body?"

"Not so loud," the commissioner said. "And remember something, Charlie. I got you this job and I can bust you out of it. Maybe you are my brother-in-law, but I'll damn well break you right out of the Department."

Shannon didn't say anything.

"You know what Pealy's going to print in his newspaper?" the commissioner whispered. "He'll say you gave this kid a third degree and tortured him until the window looked like the only way out. Oh, he'll play this one up good. What a hell of a sweet mess."

Shannon wasn't listening. The poor kid, he thought. Just like Chester. Same way of pushing his hair out of his eyes. Maybe if I talked to him again . . .

The commissioner pitched his voice even lower. "I've got it, Charlie," he said. "The Lobetz killing."

"What about it?"

"Don't you get it? Look. We pin the Lobetz killing on him. Simple. And it's a feather in your cap, and in the Department's too."

Shannon stared at him.

The commissioner grinned. "The Lobetz killing didn't go down anyway. He had a lot of friends and they're all yelling for the punk who held up his store and knocked him off. You get it now?" He nodded toward the window. "That kid out there confessed, then tried to escape."

"Forget it, Tom," Shannon said. "The kid would deny it, and he'd probably come up with an alibi."

"How's he going to deny it, when he's dead?" the commissioner asked softly.

"And suppose he doesn't jump?"

The commissioner's smile faded. "He's got to jump. We'll make him jump."

"Get the hell out of here," Shannon said.

"Now wait a minute, Shannon. I—"

"You heard me," Shannon said. "Get out."

"Why, you ungrateful bastard," the commissioner said. "What the hell were you before I yanked you up to where you are? And God knows I'd never have done that if you hadn't married my own sister, and she begging me —"

"I said to get the hell out," Shannon said, and got to his feet.

The commissioner was smiling again, another kind of smile now. "All right, Charlie," he said. "I'll go. But you've had it. No matter what happens now, I'm going to bust you out of the Department. So help me God, I'll have your job by Monday morning!" He turned and strode to the door.

"I don't think it will be much longer, sir," the uniformed cop at the window said.

The priest spoke to Shannon but his eyes were on the floor. "I'm afraid the poor lad has made up his mind. I — I've done everything I can . . . everything."

Shannon turned to Sergeant Bailey. "Get me a rope," he said. There's a hardware store around the corner on Walnut. Get down there as fast as you can and bring me about thirty feet."

"Right," Bailey said, and ran toward the door.

"What are you going to do?" the priest asked.

"I'm going out there after him."

"I don't believe he'll let you near him."

"He'll let me," Shannon said. "I'll just keep talking to him. I know how to talk to boys like that, Father. I've got one of my own."

Shannon tied the rope around his thick waist and crawled out onto the ledge.

"Don't come any closer," Paul Merton said. "If you do, I'll jump."

"We know you didn't kill anyone," Shannon said. "But we've got to get you inside so we can talk it over." He inched along the slanting granite ledge.

"I told you how it was," Paul said. "I was supposed to meet Mr. Sorrentino in Montgomery." His thin body was tense and his face was so pale that Shannon could see the pink tracery of the tiny veins beneath the surface of the skin.

"Sure, Paul," Shannon said. "Just take it easy, son."

"Mr. Sorrentino took a train and I drove his car. He wanted to use it in Montgomery, but he said he couldn't get any sleep on a long car trip like that, and so he wanted me to drive the car there for him."

"My boy Chester's about your age, Paul," Shannon said, moving along the ledge very slowly now. "You and him —"

"Don't come any closer!" Paul said tightly.

"Easy now, Paul . . ." Shannon said, and took another cautious step.

Then he saw Paul's rigid body tilting away from the wall of the building. "No, Paul!" he yelled, and reached out for him.

His clawing hand skidded across Paul's thin shoulders. He felt his fingers twisting in the cloth of his shirt. Then there was the sound of cloth ripping, and suddenly Shannon's hands were holding nothing.

As Paul's body hurtled downward, one of his feet slammed hard against the side of Shannon's head, and Shannon felt himself slipping. He tried to grasp the narrow ledge, but it was too late.

For one long moment he could feel himself falling. Down below, the mass of tiny faces looked up at him, revolving slowly as his body twisted in the air.

Then there was the sickening wrench of the rope around his waist as it stopped his fall. There was pain. Pain that burst in his stomach and flooded through his body and made him unconscious.

Shannon lay on the floor of room 607. He opened his eyes very slowly, while awareness returned to him and the room was suddenly filled with light and voices.

"The . . . the boy," he said. "He's dead?"

The priest nodded.

"You took a hell of a chance on your life," Sergeant Bailey said. There was a new respect in his voice. "My God, Chief . . ."

"I had to do it," Shannon said. "I had to. You know that, Bailey." He tightened his stomach muscles against the pain. It was worth it, he thought. The kid was innocent. It was worth a chance on my life; it was worth losing my job.

"The doctor's on his way," the priest said.

"Chief, I got to tell you something," Sergeant Bailey said.

Shannon turned his eyes toward him. "What is it?" he asked weakly. He was thinking about the kid out on the ledge. If he had only been a little faster . . . if he'd only grabbed for him a little sooner . . .

"We got a wire while you were unconscious, Chief," Bailey said. "They found him. Sorrentino, I mean. The Oglethorpe police found him in a swamp a couple of miles outside the city. His head was busted wide open . . . A jack handle . . ." He looked away from Chief Shannon, toward the open window. "The kid's fingerprints were all over it."

Then, they were all quiet for a long while, until Chief Shannon said:

"I didn't think he did it, Bailey."

"No," Bailey said.

"He was just a kid," Chief Shannon said.

"You never can tell," Bailey said shortly.

"No. You can't ever tell, can you?"

And the priest straightened and walked toward the door, his lips moving silently.

Classification: Dead

BY RICHARD MARSTEN

Sheryl had been a beautiful woman. Now she was a very ugly corpse.

O'Hara was on the desk when I came in. I stopped to chat with him for a moment, and then I asked, "Is Freddie in yet?"

"Upstairs," he said.

I took the elevator up to Homicide, stopped to talk to the Skipper in the corridor, and then walked in to find Freddie with his customary second cup of coffee in his fist.

"Want some joe?" he asked. "It's fresh."

It was a ritual we went through. Every morning, Freddie asked me if I wanted some coffee, and every morning I told him I'd already had some. I told him that now, and he nodded and went back to his quiet sipping.

I let him sip for a few minutes, looking through the window at the people with their collars raised, their steps quick against the cold.

"The autopsy come in yet?" I asked. I didn't turn from the window.

"Yep," Freddie said.

"What'd they say?"

"Like we figured. The slug took her in the heart. Killed her instantly."

"And the other thing?"

"Yeah, that too," Freddie said.

"What do you mean, that too?"

Freddie turned his eyes to the coffee cup, almost as if he were embarassed. "She'd been through an abortion. She . . . she was still bleeding internally when she was killed."

"But it wasn't the cause of death."

"No. The bullet killed her."

"Has she been identified yet?"

"The boys are working on that now. It should be fairly simple, Rick. Her clothes were all tailor-made, Hattie Carnegie label."

I whistled softly.

"You're not surprised, are you? She looked like class."

I nodded. "Except class doesn't wind up in Central Park with a bullet in the chest."

Freddie shrugged. "Bullets don't respect class," he said philosophically.

"You got the report on the slug?" I asked.

"On your desk."

I walked to my desk and picked up the card there. I'd seen a thousand of them, and this one was no different than the rest. I scanned it quickly.

BULLET

CALIBRE .38	WEIGHT 158 GRMS.
TWIST 16 inches	NO. OF GROOVES 6
WIDTH OF LAND MARKS	.057
WIDTH OF GROOVE MARKS	.122
TYPE LEAD ———	METAL CASE No
HALF METAL ———	SOFT POINT No
DECEASED Unidentified	
DATE November 9, 1953	
REMARKS: Colt Special bullet taken from heart of unidentified female.	
	D.D. 83

"That gives us a hell of a lot," I said.

"You're getting impatient again," Freddie said. "I can always tell when you're getting impatient."

"Go to hell," I told him.

"What's so special about this broad?" Freddie asked suddenly.

"Nothing," I said. "Except she's pretty maybe. I hate to see a pretty woman wind up looking ugly. This one had class, Freddie, right down to her toes. I can see her sitting in the Stork Club, maybe, with a cocktail in her hands. She's slim, and proud, and beautiful."

"She's dead," Freddie said dispassionately.

"I know. That's what hurts, Freddie. She shouldn't be dead."

Freddie said nothing. Then, after a long while, he asked, "I guess we'll have to wait until she's identified."

"I guess so," I said.

We sat down to wait.

We didn't have to wait long. The report came in a while later. The clothes had been tailored especially for her, and they were extremely simple to trace, a matter of merely checking back through the records of the firm. The clothes had been tailored for a Mrs. Sheryl Snyder, and her last address was 1112 Riverside Drive.

Freddie and I checked out an RMP, but when we got to the last known address, there was no Snyder listed in the hall directory. We inquired with the superintendent of the building and also with the elevator boy. They both said Mr. and Mrs. Snyder had moved in September, and they'd left no forwarding address. We went back to the radio motor patrol car.

"At least there's a *Mr.* Snyder," Freddie said.

"Yeah."

"We'll check the directories when we get back to the office."

"Sure," I said. We drove slowly, with the cold outside the car. I felt safe and protected in the car, like a bear settling down for the Winter, no worries, no nothing. I didn't feel like getting out when we reached the station, but I did anyway, and we went upstairs to the office.

There was a report from the MPB when we got there, and that saved us a trip to the phone directories.

"Missing Persons Bureau," I said to Freddie.

"Yeah?"

"Call clocked in at 10:27. From a Mr. Alfred Snyder, 812 East Eighty-Sixth Street."

"Snyder, huh?"

"Yeah. Says his wife's been gone since yesterday morning. Says he's worried frantic."

Freddie sighed and shrugged into his jacket. "Upstairs and downstairs," he said. "That's all we do. Upstairs and downstairs."

"Come on," I said.

The apartment building was a swank one, with a long lemon-colored awning stretching to the sidewalk, and a doorman with a lot of gold braid on his chest. The doorman held open the door for us, and Freddie and I walked in, checked the directory, and then headed for the elevator banks. We took the car up to the twelfth floor, looked for apartment 12-C, and then pressed an ivory stud in the door jamb. We heard a hum inside the apartment, and then the muted sound of footsteps on a thick rug. The peephole in the door clanked open, and I held up my buzzer.

"Police officers," I said.

The door opened instantly. A silver-haired man stood there, his face burned with a Florida tan, his eyes a piercing blue. He had a regal nose and thin lips, and he held his cleft chin high. He was the kind of guy you expect to see in a Man of

Distinction ad. He was Class with a capital C, and he matched the dead Mrs. Snyder perfectly, except perhaps in age. I judged him to be pressing fifty, and Sheryl Snyder couldn't have been more than 32.

"Mr. Snyder?" I asked.

"Yes," he said in a businesslike manner. "You're answering my call, aren't you?"

"Yes," I said. "May we come in?"

"Certainly. Certainly." He held the door wide, and Freddie and I followed him into a drop living room. The place was expensively furnished, as I figured it would be, and Snyder walked to a grand piano in one corner, taking a Parliament from a hammered silver box and lighting it quickly.

"I'm Detective-Sergeant Richard Silverstein," I said. "This is my partner, Detective-Sergeant Andrews."

Snyder nodded politely. "How do you do?"

Freddie pulled out his pad and tweaked his nose. I cleared my throat. This was going to be the hard part, but it had to be passed.

"I'm sorry to bring you bad news, sir," I said. "But . . ."

Snyder's eyebrows went up a little. "What is it? Is it Shirley? Has anything . . ."

"She's dead, sir."

The air seemed to go out of Snyder. His shoulders slumped, and his backbone sagged, and he repeated dully, "Dead."

"Yes, sir. She was shot to death with a .38 Colt Special bullet. We found her in Central Park last night."

"You . . . you were the ones who found her?"

"No, sir. The beat man. I used 'we' to mean the police."

"I . . . I see."

"I'm sorry, sir."

"That's . . . that's all right. I mean . . . it's only your job."

"Yes, sir."

He shook his head and stared at the glowing end of his cigarette. "Have they . . . have you found who did it yet?"

"No, sir. We're working on that now."

"It doesn't seem possible, does it? Shirley . . ."

I interrupted him. "We have her name as Sheryl, sir. Is that incorrect?"

"Yes, yes, I keep forgetting. Shirley is right. It started as Shirley, then she began spelling it Shirlee, and from that it became Sheryl. I suppose most of our friends know her as Sheryl."

"I see."

"What time did she leave here yesterday, sir?" Freddie asked.

"In the morning. Very early. About eight, I should say."

"Did she tell you where she was going?"

"No. Yes, yes she did. She said she had some shopping to do. I was ready to leave for the office, so I didn't pay much attention."

"What sort of work do you do?"

"Export-Import. Dates mostly."

"I see. How old are you, sir?"

Snyder looked at me curiously. "Forty-seven."

"And Mrs. Snyder?"

"Thirty-four."

"Any children, sir?"

"No."

"Do you own a gun, Mr. Snyder?"

"No."

I looked at him squarely. "Did you know your wife was pregnant, Mr. Snyder?"

"Yes," he said softly.

"Did you know she had an abortion?"

It had a sort of delayed reaction. He took a puff on his cigarette, let out a wreath of smoke, and then his hand began shaking, and his mouth fell open, and more smoke dribbled over his lip.

"What?" he stammered. "What?"

"Yes, sir. We have every reason to believe she underwent an illegal abortion sometime yesterday."

"An abort . . . an abortion!" Snyder shook his head. "No. No, you must be mistaken. She surely would have told me. I mean . . . an abortion! Shirley? No, no." He kept shaking his head.

"You didn't know about this, then?"

"No, I did not. I can't believe it. I . . ."

"She never discussed her plans for an abortion?"

"No, she didn't."

"Was there any trouble between you, sir?" Freddie asked.

"No. No trouble at all. We were very happy."

"Then how come you didn't know about the abortion? That's the sort of thing a woman talks over with her husband."

Snyder took a hasty drag on his cigarette. "I . . . this seems a rather indelicate matter to . . ."

"Did you, or didn't you know?"

"I *did not* know. I already told you that." He seemed a little angry now.

"We're just trying to get at the facts, sir," Freddie said.

"Well, you seem to be taking a rather circuitous route!" Snyder said.

"I'm sorry, sir," I said.

Snyder subsided sullenly, and Freddie asked "Do you have a family doctor? And if so, may we have his name and address?"

"Certainly. Dr. Lawrence Dowling. On East Eighty-Fourth. I forget the exact address."

"You're tanned, sir," I said. "Were you in Florida recently?"

"Yes. Shirley and I returned only a few weeks ago. We gave up our old apartment when we went down, and we moved into this one on our return."

"Does your wife keep an appointment book?" Freddie asked.

"No."

"Mmm. Well, I guess that does it," I said.

"We'll let you know if we get anything, Mr. Snyder," Freddie said. Then, very diplomatically:

"You weren't planning on any out-of-town business, were you?"

"No."

"Fine. We'll want to contact you."

We said our goodbyes, and when we were going down in the elevator, Freddie asked, "What do you think?"

"He seemed properly grieved," I said. "And properly indignant. He seemed very proper."

"A proper Papa," Freddie cracked. "Who didn't know about the abortion."

"Maybe Dr. Dowling knows," I said.

We stopped off at the office first, checking on applications for pistol permits. Snyder had never applied for one. That meant nothing, of course. The Federal Firearms Act is probably the most maligned law in the nation. We stopped in at the lab, and the boys there were still compiling the data and photos on where the dead Mrs. Snyder had been found. We left them and went to see Dr. Lawrence Dowling.

He looked like Errol Flynn, right down to the carefully groomed mustache under his nose. He was immaculately handsome in his white tunic, and he admitted us to his office and shook our hands when we introduced ourselves. He walked to his desk then, picked up a gold pencil and held it in his hands like the handle and pointed tip of a sword whose temper he was testing.

He was very handsome, this Dr. Dowling. He was also sporting a fresh Florida tan.

"What can I do for you, gentlemen?" he asked. His voice was cultured, and he smiled when he spoke.

"Sheryl Snyder," Freddie said. "Was she a patient of yours?"

"Yes," Dr. Dowling said. He smiled pleasantly.

"She's dead," I told him. "We have reason to believe she went through an abortion on the day she was killed. Did you know she was pregnant?"

I guess it was too much for him all in one breath. A murder, an abortion, and a pregnancy, all tossed at him together. He blinked his eyes a little, and I thought sure as hell he would say, "I beg your pardon." He didn't. He just sat there blinking until Freddie repeated, "Did you know she was pregnant?"

"Why . . . why, no. No. My God, who'd have suspected? Dead? An abortionist killed her?"

"A bullet killed her," I said. "Maybe the abortionist for some reason, maybe not. You didn't know she was pregnant?"

"No. No, I didn't."

"You just come back from Florida?" Freddie asked.

Dr. Dowling hesitated. "Yes," he said.

"You didn't happen to run across Mrs. Snyder down there, did you?"

Dr. Dowling hesitated again. He sighed deeply, like the hero in a tragedy. "Yes, I did."

"Professionally?" Freddie asked.

"I . . ." Dr. Dowling sighed again. "I suppose the truth will help you."

"She was murdered," Freddie said.

"No, I didn't see her professionally."

"Socially then?"

Dr. Dowling hesitated again. But beneath his hesitation, I sensed that he wanted to talk. He was a kiss-and-teller, and he'd kissed, and now he wanted to tell. All he needed was a little pushing, and Freddie supplied that.

"If you were playing with her, that's your business," he said. "We're only interested in her murderer."

"We . . . we knew each other quite well," Dr. Dowling said.

"Well enough to know whether she was pregnant or not? Socially, I mean, not professionally."

"Yes, well enough." Dr. Dowling smiled. "To tell the truth, I never even thought of it. Sheryl . . ."

"Sheryl *what?*"

"Sheryl was a rather wild person. I mean . . . well, I can't flatter myself into believing I was the only one." The look on his face told us he'd have liked very much to believe that.

"There were others then?"

"Yes. Many others, I believe. That is, Sheryl made no secret of it. She . . . she talked freely of the other men she'd known."

Freddie glanced at me, and I knew he was thinking about what I'd said earlier. *Class.*

"Did her husband know about all this?"

"I couldn't say." Dr. Dowling smiled a superior smile. "The husband is usually the last to know, isn't he?"

"But you never suspected she was pregnant. Not all the time you knew her."

"No. You'll pardon me, but Sheryl . . . well, she hardly seemed the type of woman . . . that is, there are some women who are cut for the pattern of motherhood. Being a mother would have tied her down considerably. I don't think Sheryl would have liked it."

"I see," I said.

"And . . ." Dr. Dowling paused. "Sheryl was very . . . very proud of her body . . . very aware of . . . well, she was a physical person. She first came to me on recommendation, with a bruise on her left breast. She wanted it taken care of immediately."

"And you took care of it," Freddie said sarcastically.

The doctor let this roll off his back. "A woman like that . . . so conscious of her freedom . . . and so aware of her physical appearance . . . well, pregnancy is a rather deforming thing. I'm not at all surprised she sought an abortionist."

"But she never discussed this?"

"Hardly. I'm afraid I don't know any abortionists."

Freddie raised his eyebrows dubiously. "Who was the person who recommended her, doctor?"

"Linda Carson." He stroked his jaw thoughtfully. "I wish we didn't have to drag her into this, though."

"Why not?"

"Well, Linda and I . . . that is . . ."

"When do you find time for your practice?" Freddie asked blankly. "Let's have her address, doctor."

Dr. Dowling became all business. "Certainly." He buzzed his receptionist and asked her for Linda Carson's records, even though I was sure he knew her address from memory. While we waited, I asked, "Miss or Mrs.?"

"Linda?" Dr. Dowling smiled to let us know everything was aboveboard in this instance. "Miss." When the records came, he gave us her address, and we thanked him for his cooperation, and then left. We had lunch in a little pharmacy on Lexington Avenue, and then went looking for Linda Carson, Miss.

She was a beautiful woman, but in a harsh, carefully calculated way. She opened the door for us after we flashed our buzzers, and we immediately got that feeling of hardness that no hair dresser or beauty salon can quite take away. She had a narrow face, with deep brown eyes and black brows. Her lips were tinted a bright scarlet, and she was wearing her hair in the new Italian cut, shaggy and curling around her face. She was obviously dressed to go out, with a low-cut silk job that had wide shoulders and almost no front. A diamond clip held whatever front there was together, nestling in the shadowed valley of her bunched breasts. She fingered her hair momentarily, then suddenly remembered we were cops and not to be classed with ordinary men.

"What is it?" she asked.

"A few questions," Freddie said. "May we come in?"

"I was just leaving."

"We won't be long."

"Well . . ." She hesitated, then stepped back out of the doorway. "All right, but it'll have to be fast."

We followed her into a nicely furnished apartment, and she went to a low coffee table. There were two purses on the table, and she began changing the junk from one purse to another. She leaned over while she worked, and Freddie riveted his eyes to the front of her dress, and I knew he was thinking you could find her kind — minus the veneer and the expensive clothes and jewelry — in night court on any day of the week, and twice on Saturdays. Freddie smelled that on her, and his eyes narrowed. I smelled it, too, so I got right to the point.

"Have you seen the papers today, Miss Carson?"

"Yes," she said, busy with the purses.

"You know that Sheryl Snyder is dead?"

"I know."

"You were a friend of hers, weren't you?"

"Yes, I was."

"Did you know she was pregnant?"

"Yes. I knew."

"When did she tell you?"

"Two months ago, I guess. Something like that."

"Did you recommend Dr. Dowling to Mrs. Snyder?" Freddie asked.

She hesitated. "Yes, I did."

"Why?"

"He's a good doctor. Sheryl had a . . . a bruise. I told her to see Larry about it. Dr. Dowling, that is."

"Do you know him well?"

"Very well. Larry and I see a lot of each other. Socially." She paused and said, "Let's move on to the next question if we're going to keep playing District Attorney."

Freddie was getting sore. I could see it in the set of his mouth, and in the way he kept clenching and unclenching his hands.

"When Mrs. Snyder told you she was pregnant," he said, "did she also tell you she didn't like the idea?"

"I guess she mentioned something about it. No woman likes being all bloated up. Especially a pretty woman." To emphasize her point, she sucked in a deep breath, and Freddie's eyes flicked momentarily to the diamond clip between her breasts.

"Did she mention what she planned to do about it?"

Linda Carson eyed Freddie steadily. "I don't know what you mean," she said.

"Let's not play Baby-Blue Eyes," Freddie said disgustedly.

She turned to me and said, "You should teach your partner some manners."

"Did you send her to Dowling when she told you she was pregnant?" Freddie asked.

"No. Larry's not an obstetrician."

"Is he an abortionist?"

"Don't be absurd!"

"Did Snyder like the idea of his wife being pregnant?"

"He liked it fine. The old bastard liked it fine. What man doesn't like it? It took Sheryl out of the field, and it meant an heir for him. There isn't a man who doesn't like it."

"Was it his kid?" Freddie asked abruptly.

"You have a filthy mind, don't you?" Linda Carson asked.

"Murder is a filthy business. Your friend Larry already told us that Mrs. Snyder wasn't exactly a symbol of purity."

"Well, take your mind out of the gutter. It was Snyder's kid, all right."

"How do you know?"

"Sheryl said it was. She ought to have known."

"Do you think it might not have been Snyder's?"

"No." She paused. "Sheryl knew and liked a lot of men — but she was a careful kid. Damned careful."

"Did you know she went to an abortionist?"

"No," she said quickly.

"She did," Freddie said. "On the

day she was killed. Wouldn't you call that a strange coincidence?"

"I suppose so," she said wearily.

"I'd say it was a stranger coincidence that she was very buddy-buddy with Dr. Dowling, and that he didn't even know she was pregnant. I'd say it was strange for a doctor who knew her as well as her husband to . . ."

"Leave Larry out of this," Linda Carson said abruptly. "Don't drag his name into this. He didn't know a thing about it."

"Then you did know she was planning an abortion!"

"Larry had nothing to do with it," she said.

"Did you know Larry was very chummy with Mrs. Snyder?"

Linda Carson sucked in a deep breath. "Yes," she said softly. "So what? I'm no goddamned angel, either. Larry and I have an understanding. But he had nothing to do with any abortion."

"Who did?" Freddie asked.

"I don't know."

"Look," I said, "we're trying to find a killer. We can hold you as accessory after, and we can make the good Dr. Dowling sorry he ever knew a woman who had an abortion. Now . . ."

"Larry's clean," she said. "Please leave him out of it."

"Sure. What's the butcher's name?"

"Fields," she said quickly. "Amos Fields."

"M.D.?"

"No. I don't think so."

"Do you know his address?"

"Yes."

"What is it?"

She gave it to us, and Freddie jotted it down in his pad.

"Did you send Mrs. Snyder to him?" I asked.

"Yes," she said softly.

"Why?"

"Because she didn't want a goddamned baby. You don't know what it's like. You don't know what it's like to see your stomach get all bloated, and your breasts sagging to your knees."

"That's the good reason. What's the real one?"

Linda Carson sighed. "She promised to stay away from Larry if I helped her. She . . . she was desperate. You . . . you don't know what it's like."

Freddie looked at her and smiled a little. "Do *you*, Miss Carson?"

"Get the hell out of here," she said. "You've got what you want now."

We left.

We put a stakeout on Amos Fields' place, keeping it under constant surveillance for two days. On the third day, we hit it.

There was a young girl on his table, and she couldn't have been more than sixteen. We collared Fields, and then sent for an ambulance to take care of the girl. Even with the girl on the table, even with a bloody scalpel in his hands, Fields protested it wasn't an abortion.

He kept singing the same song under the lights downtown. He was a small nervous man with trembling hands, and every time I thought of a woman under those hands in an operation, I wanted to strangle him. He kept wiping the back of one hand across his runny nose, and even that mannerism made me angry. We kept him under the lights, with the Skipper looking in every now and then, and finally he cracked.

"What about Sheryl Snyder?"

"I . . . I don't know any Sheryl Snyder," Fields said.

"You performed an abortion on her five days ago," we told him.

"No. No, I didn't."

"We know you did. We got the dope from another one of your patients."

"I don't have any patients. This girl you saw on the table, she was the first one."

"I thought you said she had appendicitis."

"No," he said gravely. "No, I never said that."

"You did. You said she begged you to operate."

"She did. She did beg me."

"For an abortion?"

"Yes." Fields raised himself up with dignity. "Abortions should be legal."

"Did you feel that way when you operated on Mrs. Snyder?"

"No. I didn't operate on any Mrs. Snyder."

"Linda Carson says you did. She was a patient of yours, too, wasn't she?"

Fields swallowed hard. "I . . . all right, I did Mrs. Snyder. But I had nothing to do with her getting killed. Nothing at all."

"You know she was killed?"

"I saw it in the papers. I had nothing to do with it. When she left me, she was fine. I swear it."

"She had internal hemorrhages, our docs say."

"Well, that may be. That's a risk. If abortions were legal, there wouldn't be that risk. But I didn't kill her. It wasn't me who put that bullet in her."

"Do you own a gun, Fields?"

"Yes. A Colt .45. I got it in the Army."

"Do you have a permit for it?"

"Yes."

"We can check that, you know."

"Go ahead, check it. Anyway, the papers said a .38 killed her. You can't fire a .38 slug from a .45. Go ahead, check it."

"What time did she leave you, Fields?"

"About four in the afternoon."

"Where'd she go?"

"Home. Where else?"

"What do you mean, home?"

"I called a cab for her. When the cabbie came, she was very weak. I helped her in, and I gave him the address."

"What address?"

"812 East Eighty-Sixth Street. That's where she lives."

"You're sure about that?"

"Of course I am." He paused and then pursued his favorite subject. "Abortions should be legal, that's what. This sneaking around stinks. Abortions should be legal. It's a crime, I tell you."

"You're right there, Fields," Freddie said.

We checked on Fields' permit, and he sure as hell did have one for a Colt .45. We went down to the lab then to see if they had anything for us. They told us a lot.

"We figure time of death at about six P.M.," Sanossian said.

"So early, huh? She wasn't found in the park until eleven or so."

"Yeah. Well, that figures. She wasn't killed in the park."

"What?"

Sanossian nodded. "The slug was in her heart, Rick. A coronary wound, lots of blood. There wasn't enough blood where we found her to keep a mosquito alive."

"Then you figure she was killed elsewhere and dumped in the park."

"Couldn't be any other way," Sanossian said.

"You getting an idea?" I asked Freddie.

"I'm getting a big one," he said. "Let's get to work."

When he answered the door, he looked as impeccable as ever, as unruffled, as poised, as dignified. He said, "Ah, gentlemen," and then led us into his living room.

"Have you found anything?" he asked.

"A few things," I said.

"Good, good."

"Not too good, Mr. Snyder," I told him.

He looked at me curiously, but said nothing.

"First," I said, "we checked with your office about a half-hour ago. They said you hadn't come in on the day of your wife's death. You told us you were leaving for the office when she went 'shopping' that morning."

"I . . . oh yes, I remember. It was such a lovely day, I decided to stay out. I . . ."

"It was cloudy on the day your wife was killed, Mr. Snyder."

A frown puckered his forehead.

"Second, the abortionist who operated on your wife told us he put your wife in a cab after the operation. This was at four o'clock or thereabouts. He gave the cabbie this address. We checked with the cab companies in the city, Mr. Snyder. A pickup was made at Field's address on that day at four-twelve. Your wife was dropped in front of this apartment at four-fifty-two. She was killed at about six."

"I don't understand. What are you trying to . . ."

"I'll spell it, Mr. Snyder. You didn't go to work that day. You knew your wife was planning an abortion, and you'd probably warned her against it. She was playing with every guy and his brother, and you probably figured a child would put an end to that. You also wanted a baby. You're no spring chicken, Mr. Snyder. You wanted that kid."

"Really, I . . ."

"She probably told you she was going ahead with the abortion. It wasn't something she'd tell any of her lovers about, Mr. Snyder. Even Dr. Dowling didn't know she was pregnant, and he was a medical man. You followed her to the abortionist, and then you came home, boiling inside, thinking of the years you'd played the cuckold, and now thinking of this last blow. You let it build up until she came home that night."

"I . . . no, you're wrong. I didn't know she was planning an abortion."

"You knew, Mr. Snyder. You knew, and Linda Carson knew—but the cabbie brought your wife *here* after the operation. It was here that she was killed."

"No. No, I didn't. . . ."

"You waited until dark, and then you brought her body to the park. You probably used your own car, and we can check that, Mr. Snyder, and we'll damn well find blood stains, you can bet on that. Now how about it? How about it, Mr. Snyder?"

He washed his hand over his face, and then quietly said, "Yes. Yes, I killed her. I wanted that baby very much. She had no right to . . . you see, I knew of her activities, I knew of the other men. A baby would have . . . and I wanted it, I told her I wanted it. I told her not to go . . . go through with the abortion. She . . . she laughed at me . . . she . . . I killed her! She deserved it! She killed my baby!"

Snyder leaned against the piano, and I waited for a long while before I said, "You'd better come along with us, sir."

"Yes," he said. "Yes." He moved off the piano, with his head bent and his shoulders hunched. I looked at him, and he said, "I still have the gun, if you want it. I still have it." He paused and then looked at me curiously. "Maybe I should have got rid of it."

"Maybe your wife shouldn't have," I said.

I wasn't talking about the gun.

Long Way to KC

DICKIE COSMOS went to Greenview on vacation for two reasons. In the first place, he had just enough money to pay train fare that far from Kansas City. In the second place, Greenview was a burg Buck Finney wouldn't be caught dead in, and this increased Dickie's chances of not being caught there in an identical condition.

It started in a poker game in Finney's hotel room. They were playing five card draw, Jacks or

The gal was stacked, and her husband had a pile of dough. What more could a guy like Cosmos ask for?

BY FLETCHER FLORA

better and no limit, and Dickie drew one card to two pairs and filled a house. He was holding aces and eights. This combination is well known in the folklore of Americana as the dead man's hand, and that's the way it turned out for Dickie. He backed the full house in a succession of raises and counter-raises to the amount of a cool grand in the face of Finney's straight flush, and he wound up dead. Figuratively, that is, with a good prospect for making it literal.

This was because he'd been betting the hand and nothing else. He didn't have the grand. He hung on desperately, hoping to recoup, but he only doubled his deficit. When the game broke up, he turned his charm on and his pockets out. His handsome face and the palms of his hands were clammy, but he put on a pretty good front. Unfortunately, however, Big Finney was impervious to fronts, even charming ones. He looked at Dickie across the poker table, and his own face was like something left over from the Paleolithic Age.

"You welshing, Dickie?"

"No, Buck. Hell, no. I just need a little time, that's all."

Finney built a neat little stack of blue chips and then knocked it over with a flip of his thick fingers. The chips clattered and rolled, and Dickie wondered if the gesture was supposed to be significant. He decided that it was, and the cold sweat glistened on his smooth face.

"Sure, Dickie," Finney said. "I'll give you time. I'll give you just twenty-four hours."

Dickie looked stricken. "Twenty-four hours isn't much time to raise two grand, Buck."

Finney shrugged and said, "I'm giving you a break. It's for the sake of the dames, Dickie. I wouldn't want to break their hearts if I could help it."

It was true that Dickie knew a lot of dames. He usually managed to live pretty well on their collective donations, as a matter of fact. None of them had two grand, however, and after eighteen hours had passed without any appreciable improvement in his financial condition, Dickie checked schedules at Union Station and caught the train south to Greenview.

He didn't even have the nominal price of a room in the town's solitary hotel. It was a dismal clapboard dump, anyhow, and Dickie took a dim view of being its guest, even on a non-paying status. While he was trying to figure an angle, he wandered out of town along a narrow, rocky road. This was Ozark country, and all around him the earth lifted ancient bones bristling with scrub oak. Farm buildings cling precariously to the slopes of hills and ridges.

Dickie walked quite a way, mostly uphill, it seemed, and after a while he was aware that his feet were burning like hell inside his narrow shoes. Moreover, he was as dry as a bag of popcorn, and he wanted a drink of water. Turning off onto a private drive that climbed to the yard of a shabby farmhouse, he labored up and looked around for a well. Spotting it off behind the house a short distance, he went back and helped himself. The water was sweet and cold, and he sat down on the well cap to smoke a cigarette, feeling somewhat better.

It was then he saw the dame. She came out the back door of the house and stood on the porch looking across the yard at him. She was wearing a man's blue work shirt, open at the throat, and a pair of jeans that were too big for her and must have belonged to the same man who contributed the shirt. The outfit did nothing for her, but Dickie had a sharp eye for dames, and he could see that there was a nice distribution of good stuff underneath. She had dark, tangled hair with enough natural curl to minimize its unbrushed condition, and her face was the soft, heavy type that would someday become gross, though now, in its brief prime, it possessed a kind of full, sulky sensuality that was more vital than beauty. Feeling within himself a strong stirring of interest, Dickie lifted a hand in greeting and projected his charm.

"I helped myself to a drink. Do you mind?"

She came down off the porch and crossed the yard. Watching her come, detecting the lines and motion of her body inside her loose clothes, he felt his interest intensify and acquire an abortive purposiveness.

"It's all right. You can have all the water you want."

Her voice suited her body. Heavily sensual, throaty, it achieved the effect of a caress that was as tangible as the intimacy of fingers. Dickie stepped up the voltage of his smile, flashing enamel and lifting an eyebrow in a practiced boyish expression.

"My name's Cosmos. Dickie Cosmos. I just walked out from town."

"I'm Rose Flannery. From Greenview?"

"That's right."

She sat down beside him on the well cap, and he noticed a petulant droop to her full lower lip. She hiked the loose legs of her jeans up over her knees, exposing slim ankles, slightly soiled, that swelled upward in beautiful calf lines.

"I don't blame you for walking out," she said. "Greenview's a damn good town to be from."

Oh, oh, he thought. A discontented dame. A restless rustic lovely. What could be sweeter? Or more vulnerable?

"It didn't look like much of a place," he said cautiously.

She laughed bitterly and gave him a sidewise look from under thick lashes. "Not that this rock pile is any improvement. You don't look like the kind of guy who'd be wasting his time in the sticks. You from Kansas City?"

He wondered if she should play it straight, and decided that it couldn't do any harm. As a matter of fact, he was getting a fast impression that he might have blundered onto something rare. Not as slick as the chicks around Twelfth, of course, but pretty good compensation for the time it would take a guy to figure a way out of exile.

"Yes."

"I've been to Kansas City. St. Louis, too. I liked KC better. I always planned to go back."

"It's a pretty good town, as towns go. Not as good as it used to be, though. Not like it was when Old Tom ran it."

"Just so it's a town. Just so it's got people and places."

He let his eyes drift over her obviously, and got a spontaneous reaction, a kind of instinctive stationary strutting of her body. "You look like you'd do all right in KC, baby."

"And you look like you might be able to show a girl the way. How come you're so far from home? Don't tell me you came just to see the beautiful Ozark scenery, like they talk about for the summer suckers."

"Okay. I won't tell you that."

She shrugged and lay back flat across the well cap. The faded man's shirt was pulled tight over her breasts. "Don't tell me anything, if you don't want to. A fat damn I care."

He laughed, leaning back against his braced arms. He felt a strange, warm affinity with this big country doll. He decided she'd do to play along with. Up to a point, of course.

"Just say I'm here for my health," he said.

"You in trouble?"

"You might call it that. Nothing that can't be worked out eventually. Meanwhile, I need a place to hole up in."

"You figuring to stay in that flea bag in Greenview?"

"I'm wide open to a better suggestion."

"Maybe this would be better."

She rolled her head on the well cap and slanted a look at him from hooded eyes. The pulse in his throat leaped and hammered, and his insides were shaken by silent ribald laughter. Like a school kid, he thought. Like a damn green kid with the first time coming up.

"Is that an invitation?"

"Don't you like the idea?"

"I like it, baby. I like it fine. I'm just wondering, though. It doesn't seem likely that you live here alone. Who makes the crowd?"

"Luke."

"Your husband?"

Her full lips curled. "That's one thing you could call him."

"How's Luke going to feel about me being around?"

"Don't worry about Luke. He just eats and sleeps here, and not too much of that. Most of the time he's nursing that damn broken-down still of his."

"Still? You mean they have those things down here yet? I thought they went out with prohibition."

"Maybe they did in Kansas City. Not here. Luke makes a pile of money bootlegging. Not that it does me any good. The stingy bastard's a regular miser. He loves the green stuff too much to part with any of it."

"You sure he'll let me stay around?"

"Don't worry about him, I said. I can handle it."

He stood up. "Okay, baby, you twisted my arm. I'll just hike back to Greenview and pick up the bag I left in the station there. Few things I'll need."

She didn't bother to get up. She just kept on lying there on her back on the well cap, and very slowly she extended her arms above her head, arching her spine and stretching.

"Hurry back, Dickie," she said. "Hurry right back."

He returned to Greenview, his feet still burning in his shoes, and by a kind of malicious paradox, the road that had seemed mostly uphill coming out of town seemed just as much so going back. When he reached the farm again, carrying his bag, the last of sunlight was touching only the crests of hills and ridges.

Rose was waiting for him on the back porch. Beyond her, in the lighted kitchen, he could see the figure of a man who was bent over the kitchen table spooning something into his mouth.

"Come on in the house," Rose said. "Luke's home."

He followed her into the house and set his bag on the floor inside the screen door. The man at the table stopped eating to look at him with wary little eyes, holding the spoon suspended empty between plate and mouth. Dickie felt a shock of surprise and grinned pleasantly to hide it. He'd expected a young man, but Luke was a long way past young. Fifty at least, Dickie guessed. Maybe onto sixty. He had a long, bleak face, almost rectangular in shape, with a broad, square chin. His hair was coarse and bristly, a dirty gray, and it gave more the effect of quills than hair. His voice detoured through his nose, and the nasal twang gave it a mean sound.

"What you want here?"

"I'm looking for a place to stay a few days. Your wife said maybe I could stay here."

Rose's laugh, behind him, had a jeer in it. "Luke's worried about his still. He thinks maybe you're a state agent. Maybe even a Fed."

Dickie laughed, too, just to show how funny he thought that idea was, but Luke didn't seem to think it was funny at all. His little eyes slipped past Dickie in the direction of Rose, and his bleak face was suddenly a real and considerable menace. Dickie felt an uneasy chill wriggle its way along his spine, and he realized that Luke was a dangerous man. Just as dangerous in his own way and place as a man like Buck Finney was in his.

"You shut up," Luke said. "Just keep your trap shut."

Rose repeated her laugh, but the jeer was gone, and there was something in its place that might have been the tremor of fear. Luke's eyes came back as far as Dickie and stopped. They stayed there a long time without moving.

"If you want to sleep in the barn, you can stay," he said at last. "If you don't, you can move on."

Dickie took it gracefully. "The barn's okay. I'll carry my bag down now."

Luke's spoon resumed its shuttling between plate and mouth, and Rose said, "There's a lantern in the harness room, if you want a light. Be careful of the hay."

"Sure," he said. "I'll watch it."

He carried his bag to the barn and climbed to the loft on a straight wooden ladder nailed to the inside wall. Opening the loft door, he lay in the hay in front of it and looked out to the ancient hills. He knew nothing of geology, nothing at all of the region's incredible history, but the dark remnants of earth's patient violence filled him with an indefinable unease.

Shrugging it off, he began to think of Rose, of the big ripe body in man's clothing, and after a while the threat of the hills receded. He found himself listening, expecting the soft sound of her approach up the ladder, but then he remembered the sound in her voice in the kitchen, and he decided that she wouldn't come. Not tonight. Not any time when Luke was around.

He loves the green stuff too much to part with any of it, Rose had said. The words had lingered verbatim in Dickie's consciousness. To a guy who needed two grand, they were words of considerable significance. Two grand? Better add a half. It would take a lot of interest to make Buck Finney forget that the principal of the debt was delinquent. Interest on money you owed Finney accumulated fast.

Would a billy like Luke have twenty-five C's cached? It wasn't impossible. Sometimes these hill characters surprised a guy. They were full of surprises. Take the case of a dame like Rose being hitched to a sour, ugly Ozark bootlegger like Luke, for instance. Rose was a doll with possibilities. She even talked as if she'd been to school. Maybe through a consolidated high school somewhere. Knock off the rough edges, polish her up and put her in the right rags, she'd go great along Twelfth. She'd make someone a damn sweet B-girl, at least.

It just didn't make any kind of sense, her being married to Luke. Or did it? When you considered the possibility of Luke's having a nice little green cache, things began to add up. Dickie might not know anything about geology, but he knew his share about dames, and he could recognize the predatory type a mile off. A few grand would go a long way toward getting an ambitious dame out of the hills on the right foot, and he was willing to bet dollars to tax tokens that Rose had been thinking about that when she crawled in with Luke at the start.

Lying there in the hay, looking out to where the moon was beginning to edge a distant ridge, he weighed the pros and cons of collaboration, and pretty soon he went to sleep.

He woke at daylight to sounds below. Without moving, he listened to the opening and closing of the harness room door, the sound of heavy shoes on hard-packed earth, the opening of the barn door on the field side away from the house. Seconds later, Luke came into view, headed for the hills. He was carrying an old bolt-action rifle, and he walked with a long-legged, undulating motion that ate up the ground in a hurry.

Ten minutes passed, no longer, before Rose came up the ladder and over the hay to his side. She leaned back, braced on her elbows, her legs sprawled, and passed him a slow smile.

"Luke's gone," she said.

"I know. I watched him leave."

"You hungry?"

"A little."

"You come up to the house, I'll fix you something."

"Pretty soon. I'm in no hurry."

She looked out the loft window toward the hills into which Luke had gone, but her eyes were blank, as if they were turned inward to focus on her own thoughts. Her full lips pouted softly.

"When you going back to KC?"

He laughed. "How long does it take to get hold of twenty-five hundred bucks around here?"

She turned her head to look at him directly, and her breasts rose slowly on a deep breath to draw taut the coarse blue fabric of her shirt.

"That depends on where you look."

"It would save time to look in the right place."

"Why you need all that money to get back?"

He lifted his shoulders. "A little debt I owe to a guy who likes to be paid."

"Oh." She turned her eyes back to the hills, and she was silent for a long time. Finally she whispered, as if to herself, "I know where there's twenty-five hundred dollars. More than that. A lot more. I know just where it is."

So there it was on a tentative line. Reaching for her, he snarled fingers in her tangled hair and twisted her head around until they were exchanging long looks along a high voltage line of communication.

"I've been thinking, baby," he said. "I've been thinking about a lot of things, but mostly I've been trying to think of the reason why a nice item like you would marry Luke. Now I'm beginning to understand."

She said bitterly, "Fat lot of good it did me. I thought I could work it out of him, but I was all wrong. I sold out for nothing. After the first couple weeks, he wasn't interested in anything I had to offer. I guess he was just too old to last."

He leaned over her, his breath coming through his nose in a thin whistle. "He *must* have been old, baby. He must be a thousand."

The high voltage line contracted to zero, and minutes followed one another through the loft to the dry sound of the disturbed hay.

After a long time, she said, "Take me back to KC with you, Dickie."

He'd already anticipated that plea, and he'd decided that it had points. She'd be an interesting attachment for a while, and later on, when the thing went sour, they'd break it up, and thanks for the ride. Meanwhile, however, the whole project depended on Luke's green cache.

"I told you, baby. I can't go back without twenty-five C's."

"Luke's got it, Dickie. He must have eight, ten thousand stuck away. He's been running bootleg for a long time. You can gather a big bundle that way."

Dickie whistled softly. "Where is it?"

"In the cave. The cave where the still is. These hills are riddled with caves, you know. This one's about two miles over the way Luke went this morning, and I'm the only one besides Luke who knows about it. I followed him one day and spotted it. When he left, I went in and found the cache. All that beautiful green stuff." She held her spread fingers in front of her eyes, and her voice dripped with bitterness. "I fingered it a little. Just fingered it a little and put it back."

"How come? How come you didn't take off with it?"

She looked at him, and in her eyes was the visual equivalent of the sound he'd heard in her voice in the kitchen last night. A shiver ran through the flesh of her body.

"For the same reason you and I can't just take off with it now," she said. "Because Luke's got to be taken care of first. Don't underestimate that bastard. He's mean clear through. He's killed before, and he'd kill again. With you for company, though, I'd have the nerve to try."

"How could we get the dough and get away? You got an idea?"

"Yes." She clenched her fingers and sat looking at the fist they made. "Luke sells bootleg to a road joint a couple of miles south of here. They get Luke's stuff cheap, and it makes for big profits. I'll bet you'd be surprised how much of the stuff you buy across the bar is bootleg, even in Kansas City. This joint is Luke's biggest customer. Every Sunday Luke brings a lot of the stuff in from the cave. Sunday night, while the joint's closed, he delivers it in the truck. The point is, Luke's a three-time loser. Another rap means life. But instead, for Luke, it'll mean death. He carries an old .45

Colt revolver with him in his deliveries, and he wouldn't let himself be taken alive. You can believe that. I know Luke, and he'd never go back to the pen for keeps."

He looked at her with growing admiration. "I get it. A word to the right party, and it's good-by, Luke. Who? The sheriff?"

She shivered again. "Yes, the sheriff. Rube Wells. He hates Luke's guts. He'd love to nail him. He'd love the excuse to burn him down."

"This is Sunday, baby. By moving fast, we could do it tonight. I'd sure like to get back to KC."

"The sooner, the better."

"You got a phone here?"

"No. You'd have to go to Greenview."

"What's the name of this joint Luke delivers to?"

"The Oaks. It's just a big frame building, like a barn, but it does a lot of business."

"How does Luke get the stuff in from the still?"

"He keeps a couple mules pastured out that way. There's a cart out there, too. He brings it up in the cart."

"Okay. I better get to Greenview and back before he brings the stuff in."

"You can use the truck. Come on up to the house, and I'll fix you something to eat."

In the kitchen, he ate fat bacon and bread, washing it down with strong black coffee. Then he backed the truck out of its shed and drove to Greenview. The truck was an old 1940 pickup, shaken into a state of innumerable rattles by the rocky hill roads, and the exhaust kept popping like gunfire.

He found a telephone booth in a shabby cafe filled with the rancid odor of grease, and finally got through humming country wires to the county seat. He caught Rube Wells himself in the sheriff's office and put the finger on Luke succinctly.

The wire hummed for a few seconds after he'd finished, and then the sheriff's voice sounded harshly, "Who the hell's talking?"

"Never mind that. You want Luke Flannery or not?"

"I want him, all right."

"Then you'd better be waiting tonight on the road to the Oaks."

The voice was grim. "We'll be waiting. We'll be right there."

Dickie laughed quietly inside himself, and hung up. He laughed all the way back to the farm, and he was still laughing when he crawled out of the truck and went across the yard to the porch where Rose was waiting.

"Luke back yet?"

"No. He won't be here for a long time yet."

"Good. It's all set, baby. Neat as anything you could want."

"I hope so." That long shuddery creeping of flesh was apparent again. "I hope to God nothing goes wrong."

His eyes narrowed. "You're sure,

aren't you? About his making that delivery tonight, I mean?"

"Yes, I'm sure. He makes it regular every Sunday night. He leaves here in the truck a little before ten."

"Okay. Relax, then. We got nothing to worry about. If he doesn't go crazy, like you think, and get himself killed, he'll wind up in the county jail. Either way, it'll give you and me the chance to get the dough and get out of here."

"They got to kill him," she said. "I'll never be easy if they don't kill him. Even with life on him, I won't feel easy."

It was beginning to get dusk when Luke returned. Dickie sat in the loft and watched him come in from the hills behind a plodding mule. In the primitive two-wheeled cart, the old bolt-action rifle leaning against his knee, Luke was like something from a long way back, crude and somehow savage. In spite of himself, Dickie felt in his own flesh a shudder like the ones that had worked in Rose's. He crawled back over the hay and down the wooden ladder and stood in the open door of the barn watching Luke as he drove up and stopped.

"Long day," he said.

Luke didn't answer. He swung down off the cart and went around to the back. "You can help me unload," he said. "Put it in the truck."

There were ten cases of the stuff. A hundred and twenty quarts of raw, unlabeled, untaxed white lightning. Not expecting so large an operation, Dickie was surprised. That eight, ten grand Rose talked about was seeming more credible all the time. He worked hard at helping to transfer the load, not talking, not looking at Luke, feeling within himself a growing tensity that was part excitement and part something he couldn't define.

After the load was transferred, Luke said, "Rose'll have victuals on the table," and went off across the yard to the house. Accepting the terse statement as an invitation, Dickie followed.

The three of them sat at the table in yellow light and ate in silence. After they were finished, Luke went into the bedroom and lay down in his clothes. Dickie and Rose heard the sharp screech of old springs under his weight, and they sat looking at each other across the kitchen table with the imminent, precarious future a dark bond between them. Then Dickie shrugged and grinned and went out onto the porch, banging the screen. Sitting there on the steps, he listened to the sounds of Rose moving around behind him, scraping up the dishes.

It was funny how things happened, he thought. Couple days ago he'd been a guy with a debt and a deadly creditor. A guy from KC with a poor prognosis. Now, just like nothing, he had a hot country doll and prospects. Now, by all that was cockeyed, he stood to lift a fat bundle from a hillbilly bootlegger. He grinned in the darkness and lit a cigarette, drawing the smoke deep into his lungs.

Rose came to the screen door several times, but she didn't come out or speak. He could feel her there, charged and tense, though she was silent. It was about nine-thirty when he heard Luke's big clod-hoppers pound slowly across the kitchen floor, heard the screen door bang.

Looking up, he felt something inside him go shriveled and cold in a sudden painful contraction. Luke stood there at the edge of the porch with the yellow light of the kitchen washing his back and edging around onto the long, hard planes of his face. In his hand he held the old .45 Colt revolver. Dickie had seen plenty of guns, but he'd never seen one that looked quite so wicked as this.

"You sleep in my barn and eat my victuals," Luke said, "I guess it's only right you do a little work. You better come along and help me unload."

There was a contingency Dickie hadn't anticipated. Joke, he thought desperately. Just treat it like a very unfunny joke. He managed a laugh, forcing it through stiff lips.

"I don't think I'd be much help," he said. "I'm sleepy as a dog. Just thinking about crawling into the hay in the loft."

Luke was just holding the .45 casually, but somehow it got twisted around so that the mouth was yawning right in Dickie's face.

"I reckon you better come," Luke said.

Under that .45 calibre threat, Dickie stood up with a gaseous sensation of lightness, hysteria clouding his brain, urging him to the insanity of flight. He fought for control, crossing the yard ahead of Luke with reluctant steps, and through the cloud over his brain there penetrated in a thin whisper the words that Rose had spoken in the loft that morning: . . . *he'll never let himself be taken alive.* And he seemed to see with sudden clarity, as if his vision had achieved ascendancy over distance and night, a dark car in ambush on a dark road. Getting into the truck, he looked back toward the house and saw Rose standing frozen and immobile in the yellow rectangle of the kitchen door. Her terror reached out to him across the yard.

Slumped in the seat, he tried with desperate urgency to figure a way out. The old truck rattled and popped, fighting the hills. After a short drive, Luke wheeled it south onto a road that was a little wider, a little better graded. He handled the wheel in dour silence, the .45 rammed casually under the belt of his jeans.

"How far is it?" Dickie asked.

It hurt him to talk, the pain as actual as if he had tonsilitis. Beside him, Luke grunted.

"Up the road a piece. Not far."

They climbed a hill, rattled down into a hollow, climbed again. They crossed the crest, and the road dropped away, the truck plunging down with a fusillade of exhaust explosions.

Then, down in the hollow, the glaring spot leaped up, sweeping the truck. In the light, barely discernible, stood a man with a rifle in his hands. Luke cursed viciously, jamming brakes, and Dickie, acting at last under the grim compulsion of his last chance, tore at the door handle beside him and dove out sprawling onto the rocky road. Clawing, scrambling for the ditch in the blinding bath of light, he was aware of a confusion of sounds, shouts and explosions in a discord of violence. Something struck his shoulder, a dull impact, prompting the crazy thought that someone had hit him with a rock. He was slammed over into the ditch, rolling, and he was amazed at the force of so slight a blow.

On the road, stark in the merciless light, a guy who had everything to lose however he played it, Luke stood spraddle-legged and emptied the old Colt of its six bullets. He did it very deliberately, with spaced timing of crashing detonations, as if he were counting a long second between every pull on the trigger. When the chamber had revolved to a dead shell, he let the gun drop to the road and stood for a moment looking down at it. Then his long body folded in the middle, and went over gently onto his head and shoulders, spinning off into his back with a violent spasm of released muscles.

At that moment, Dickie was up and running. He ran blindly, relying on a sort of desperate instinct to get him back to the farm where Rose was waiting. The anesthetic of shock was gone from his smashed shoulder, and the pain was now there, growing steadily greater, eating its way like a slow fire into the rest of his body. He held the shoulder crumpled forward, the forearm below it clamped tight across his guts.

Staying away from the road, cursing and sobbing in a waste of precious breath, he ran and fell and scrambled up to keep running, and after an eternity, by a great miracle, he climbed to the farm and stood swaying in the kitchen, looking at Rose in a swirling red fog.

"God," she said. "Oh, God."

He sat down very carefully in a chair at the table and let his head fall forward onto his good arm. He began to cry again, sobs of pain and exhaustion, the crying of a stricken child. At last he raised his head and formed whispered words.

"Luke's dead," he said. "He was just like you said. Like a crazy man."

She didn't answer, and he saw then that her eyes were not on his face, where they should have been, but rather lower on his body. He looked down and saw that his entire shirt front was soaked with blood, and he could also feel the blood on his belly and legs inside his trousers. The fear in him was like a swelling icy wind as he became aware for the first time that he might really die.

"The blood," he whispered. "Stop the blood."

Apparently she didn't hear. Her eyes raised slowly, and the red fog at that moment seemed to drift out of his vision, so that he could see the eyes clearly — the compassionless calculation in them, the cold consideration of personal advantage. The advantage of the green cache unsplit.

He was filled, suddenly, with an intense, wild pity for himself. Strangely, on the edge of death, he was homesick.

And it was a long, long way to Kansas City. A way that grew longer by the second, stretching toward infinity.

Portrait of a Killer

No. 6 — Pat Mahon

BY DAN SONTUP

PAT MAHON liked to think of himself as an expert on two things — horses and women. His various systems for beating the horses never worked, but, on the other hand, his luck with the women was much better. He was a married man — had been for 14 years — and his wife had grown sort of used to Pat's wandering from the fold every now and then.

His luck stayed that way for a while — bad for the horses and good for the women. Then Pat decided to branch out and add murder to his accomplishments.

That's when his luck ran out.

It began when he met Emily Kaye, a woman who wore sneakers, played tennis, and had bulging leg muscles. Emily worked in the same office where Pat was a salesman, and the only time Pat really noticed her was the day when she asked his advice about investing some money, and he found out that she had a few thousand in the bank. After that, Pat noticed her a lot.

Emily knew that he was a married man, but that didn't stop her. It didn't stop Pat, either. He turned on all the charm in his skinny frame, spouted some poetry at Emily on a moonlit night — and that did the trick. Emily was hooked, and it didn't take Pat long to get his hands on half the money Emily had in the bank. He told her he was going to "invest" it for her, and he did just that.

Pat had a brand new system for making money on the horses, and he promptly blew all of Emily's "investment" trying to make the system work. Pat shrugged off the loss; there was still the rest of Emily's money. Trouble was, this money was in the bank, and Emily just wasn't going to part with it. So, Pat speeded up his campaign, exerted more charm on Emily, and whispered more poetry to her.

He didn't get the money, but he did receive something else — he got the news that he was going to be a father.

Emily quit her job and told Pat she wanted him to divorce his wife and marry her. Pat took her to a cottage which he had rented for the summer and tried to talk her out of the idea of marriage. Emily stood her ground. She wanted to be Mrs. Mahon, and she wanted her baby to have a legal last name. So they compromised. Emily agreed to stay on at the cottage for the summer as Pat's wife under the name of Mrs. Waller; and Pat agreed to come and visit her weekends, telling his real wife that he had to go out of town on business each weekend.

Pat spent a lot of time trying to figure a way out, and he finally reached the conclusion that his best bet was just to keep on stalling until he had talked Emily out of the idea of marrying him. But Emily now played her trump card.

She had found out that Pat had a prison record. He had once served five years for embezzlement when he had been caught stealing some money in order to keep up an affair with a woman. His wife had waited for him to serve his term, had successfully covered up his prison record, and had gotten him the salesman's job through which he met Emily.

Emily swore she'd tell Pat's boss about his prison past if he didn't start divorce proceedings against his wife right away. Pat agreed — but he had no intention of keeping the promise.

He went to work immediately on a plan to get rid of Emily. He tackled the problem with the same persistence that he used in figuring out systems on the horses, and when he had completed his plan he went out and bought something for Emily — a butcher's knife and a small saw.

Pat put the knife and saw in a suitcase and checked the whole works at the railroad station in preparation for his weekend trip to Emily. When he got there, one of the first things he did was to build a roaring fire in the fireplace. It was a warm night, and Emily was curious about the need for the fire. When she asked him about it, Pat just smiled at her and opened the suitcase and took out the butcher's knife.

Pat spent the entire weekend at his task. But he wasn't very good at it. He kept the fire going good and hot, but he found that it takes quite a bit of time and skill to burn a body bit by bit. He also found that the fire just wouldn't completely destroy a human head.

So, when Monday morning rolled around, Pat still had some of Emily left. He placed the knife and the saw back in the suitcase, added to this the remainder of Emily, closed the suitcase, and caught the early train home.

During the trip, Pat managed to open the suitcase several times, and, quietly and without being seen, toss the contents out of the train window. When he got to his destination, all that remained in the suitcase were the knife and saw and a lot of bloodstains. Pat checked the bag at the luggage counter in the station and then went on his way, a free man.

He wasn't free for long, though. A lot of little things added up very quickly. The pieces of the body had been scattered along the railroad right of way. From this, the police were able to determine the approximate location of the beginning of the train trip. Also, they noted that the calf of one leg which had been found was very well developed, indicating that the victim had been either a dancer or an athlete. A routine check of the area near where the first bit of body had been found disclosed the fact that "Mrs. Waller" had big calves and played tennis. A search of the cottage turned up some of Emily's teeth in the ashes in the fireplace. And, to add the final touch, Pat's wife found a luggage check in Pat's pocket. She had suspected for a long while now that Pat was fooling around with another woman on the weekends. So, Mrs. Mahon took the luggage check, gave it to a neighbor she trusted, and asked him to find out what her husband had checked at the railroad station.

Pat was trapped from all angles, and the net closed in quickly on him — a man who had tried hard to beat the horses and get away with murder — and failed at both.

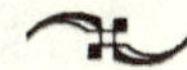

Coney Island Incident

When the girl didn't recognize Ray, it bothered him. But it bothered him a lot more when she did.

A Novelette

BY BRUNO FISCHER

I CAME OUT of the water and went searching for enough space on the beach to lie down. It wasn't easy to find. The temperature was pushing ninety-five on that Sunday afternoon in July, and the usual million people were in Coney Island. You couldn't see the sand for the bodies, all that half-naked flesh in every size and shape and color.

Near the jetty at the end of Bay 19 I found a spot.

If I didn't mind my face near the feet of a fat woman on a blanket and being tripped over every now and then by some whooping children, I could stretch out quite comfortably in the sun. I didn't like getting sand in my hair. A loose sheet of newspaper drifted on a half-hearted breeze. I snatched it and shook out the sand.

It was the first and last pages of the morning *Courier*. I could tell at a glance it was yesterday's because of the three-column headline in the lefthand corner:

ARMORED CAR HELD UP
IN BROOKLYN; BANDITS
ESCAPE WITH $80,000

For a little while Friday the robbery had interested me because it had happened a couple of blocks from our trucking concern near Bush Terminal. The armored car had been about halfway through making payroll deliveries to some of the big industrial plants when in broad daylight half a dozen or so men had shot down one guard and disarmed the other and had helped themselves to the cash in small bills. In no time the neighborhood had been crawling with cops, and two of them had been in our office questioning Mort Levy, one of our drivers, who claimed he'd seen a black Buick filled with tough-looking men driving up Fourth Avenue a few minutes after the holdup.

That was all there had been to it as far as I was concerned, and I hadn't been involved personally. The story was now no more to me than print on a newspaper which I was going to use to keep the sand off my hair.

I stretched out on my back. The sky was misty blue and the sun was a golden ball. A police helicopter, what they called an "eggbeater," flew no more than a hundred feet above the water, looking for swimmers or boaters in trouble. Somebody walked close by and kicked sand in my eyes.

When I growled, a girl muttered, "Sorry." I raised my head. She was picking her way past sprawling people and lunch baskets and deck chairs, and her head moved from side to side looking for somebody. Her bare legs were very nicely turned and her tight hips in yellow latex swung just enough.

From behind she was built something like Florence.

All of a sudden I knew I shouldn't have come here. I had thought that among a million people a man could get away from himself. But it wasn't working out that way. There were too many girls, and every now and then I was sure to see one who in some way or another reminded me of Florence. Like that girl in the yellow bathing suit.

I closed my eyes. I said to myself: Look, it's over, finished, done.

She returned your ring last night. There are other girls, thousands of pretty ones along the beach. You're not a bad looking guy and you've got that build, especially in bathing trunks, that makes a lot of them take a second look at you. Forget Florence by having some fun.

But I stayed where I was.

After a while I opened my eyes, and I found myself looking past my toes at the girl in the yellow bathing suit. I lay close to the high-tide line where the sand was packed hard and nobody was between us except a couple of small boys building a castle. She was standing at the edge of the water, a bathing cap in one hand and a striped white-and-yellow beach jacket over her arm.

I was sure I'd seen her before, many times before, but I couldn't remember where.

If she was familiar to me, I wasn't to her. Her eyes swept past me, swept slowly back and forth twice over those thousands between her and the boardwalk. This was one hell of a place to find anybody from whom you'd become separated for as much as half a minute. Her mouth twisted with annoyance, and she dropped her robe and started to put on the cap over her flaming red hair.

Then I placed her. The red hair had put me off. Last time I'd seen her, five or six years ago, it had been dark brown. She was as pretty as she'd ever been, with a button nose and a slightly turned up chin.

I sat up. "Cherry Drew," I called.

Her bare shoulders jerked, as if somebody had said *boo* to her in a dark room. Then she stared at me and stood very still with both hands fixed at the cap she had been pushing over her hair. I had an impression she was scared stiff of me — anyway, of somebody she had mistaken me for.

"Don't you remember me, Cherry?" I said. "I'm Ray Whitehead."

I'd started to move toward her, but I didn't take more than a couple of steps. Without a word or smile or any kind of acknowledgment, she picked up her beach robe and walked away along the edge of the water curling around her ankles.

I was plenty burned up. What the devil did Cherry Drew have to be snooty about? Her father had been the Hessian Valley town drunk and her mother had scrubbed people's floors to support the family and she herself had started running around with anything in pants before she was fifteen.

The hell with her. The hell with Florence. The hell with all women. I watched a big ship from Manhattan rounding the bend in the horizon at Sea Gate.

All of a sudden there was Cherry Drew coming back, and now she was smiling. "Hello, Ray," she said, putting out her hand. "For a minute I didn't recognize you."

Maybe not, but she had known who I was when I had told her my name, and I had an idea that was what had made her scoot away from me. To avoid me, or to avoid anybody who had ever known her. For some reason she had changed her mind about me, and we were shaking hands and asking each other how we were.

"Still that Tarzan build," Cherry said, lightly touching my chest with her fingertips. I tingled a little.

"Nothing wrong with *your* build," I said.

She was firm and tight all over. What I could see of her breasts swelling out of the low bodice of her strapless suit looked very good.

She had her head down and was digging in the sand with her big toe. But it wasn't really in the sand. Her toe punctured the newspaper I had spread out for my head; it went right through the headline about the armored car holdup.

"Are you with anybody?" she asked as her toe kept ripping away at that paper.

"No. And you?"

"All alone. I was getting bored." She gave me a bright smile. "Lucky I ran into you."

I wondered whom she'd been looking for and why she'd acted so nervous when she'd heard her name called.

We sat down on the sand and told each other what we'd been doing the last five years. She told me her father had died and her mother had moved in with a sister in Bridgeport and she had been working as a salesgirl in a Manhattan department store. I told her that my folks moved to Borough Park in Brooklyn while I had been in service and when I had come out of the army my father had taken me in as a partner in the small trucking business he'd established on the waterfront.

"A truck driver," she said and looked at me speculatively. "I guess you have to be pretty tough to do waterfront trucking."

"What do you know about it?"

She shrugged. "I've heard of rackets and killings on the docks."

"We keep clean," I said. "Anyway, I can take care of myself."

"I'm sure you can, Ray." She put her hand on my biceps, and again I tingled at her touch.

We hadn't much to say after that. After all, we'd never known each other well. Though Hessian Valley was a small town upstate a way, near the Hudson, where everybody knew everybody else, we'd gone with different crowds. She'd left high school after one year and at fifteen had started to run around with older men. We would say hello on the street or in juke joints, and once I'd taken her for a drive in my father's car and we'd parked and necked, but I'd been too young, too inexperienced, and probably that was why it had ended there before anything really had a chance to begin.

Now, sitting beside her among a million other people, I remembered the way her mouth had tasted more than half a dozen years ago. She had kissed more intently, more expertly, than any girl I had known. Not as sweetly as Florence, of course, but Florence hadn't —

Never mind Florence.

I jumped up. "How about a dip?"

We went in hand in hand and swam out to the ropes. As we clung to them, she said, "Did you come in a car?"

"It's in a parking lot. I'll be glad to drive you home when you're ready to leave."

She pushed herself off the ropes and let a wave carry her. I swam after her. I couldn't have met her at a better time. A man could forget a lot with a girl like her.

We were wading out of the water when one of the police helicopters passed directly over our heads. It was so low that we could see the features of the men looking down at us from the glass bubble. Cherry glanced up at them and suddenly cringed, throwing an arm across her face.

"What's the matter?" I asked.

"That thing up there startled me."

I couldn't see how she could have been startled *after* she had looked up at it.

"Let's get dressed," she said when we returned to where she had left her beach jacket.

"My clothes are in a bathhouse. What about yours?"

"I'm staying at a hotel a few blocks away."

"A hotel?" I said. "I never before heard of anybody who stayed in a hotel at Coney."

The thing about Coney Island was that you lived there all year round, or rented a room or bungalow by the week or season, or came out for the day by subway or car. If you wanted to stay at a hotel in a resort town, you went to the mountains or to some of the New Jersey beaches.

"Well, you've heard of somebody now," she snapped at me.

"But you're leaving tonight, aren't you? I mean, you want me to drive you home."

"Did I say so?" All of a sudden she sounded sore at me.

"You asked me if I had a car and I thought —"

"Don't think, Ray," she said, and gave me a very nice smile. "It's more fun not thinking."

She had something there. The whole idea of me having driven out here today was to try to stop thinking.

"Agreed," I told her. "Where do we meet when we're dressed?"

"That's easy, we're not going to separate. I'll go with you to your bathhouse and then you'll go with me to my hotel." She took my arm and said gaily, "You see, I'm not taking any chance you'll get away from me."

As we ploughed through the sand, the rich curve of her breast pressed against my arm.

I left her at the entrance to the

bathhouse. After I was dressed, I stopped off at the cashier's desk for the envelope in which I had checked my wallet and watch. I remembered the ring as I signed for the receipt. I was wearing the same tan slacks I'd worn last night when Florence had broken our engagement, and my hand flew to the fob pocket where I had angrily shoved the ring she had returned to me. It was still there — twelve hundred dollars worth of square diamond and platinum setting.

The ring meant Florence, and feeling it through the pocket brought back some of that sense of emptiness. But only some of it now. It wasn't quite as bad as it had been.

Cherry Drew was standing beside the bathhouse entrance. She had put on her striped beach jacket, and her hair was like flame under the hot sun. She didn't see me come out and when I touched her shoulder she gave a little jump. Then she drew in her breath and brought up a smile.

"You were a long time, Ray," she said, slipping her arm through mine.

On the boardwalk I bought us hot dogs. Munching them, we walked to Surf Avenue. She stopped in front of the Tunnel of Love and said, "Take me in there."

Evidently the only change in her since Hessian Valley was that she had become less subtle. She used to have a reputation for playing hard to get, even if generally at the end she wasn't. Now she hardly gave me a chance to settle in the seat before she snuggled up to me, and a moment after the boat was in the dark tunnel she took my hand and hugged it to her breast. Her mouth opened under mine.

Brief as it was, that was some ride.

From there we went into a beer parlor. We sat at a rear table and I watched her renew her face from a tiny makeup kit she took out of a pocket of her beach jacket. The color of her mouth became as vivid as her hair, and she put on too much.

I didn't care for that shade of red, and I wasn't sure I cared very much for her. She was what she had always been, a tramp. But that was all right. I was in the mood for a tramp after what a decent, respectable girl like Florence had done to me.

I acted on sheer impulse. I took the diamond ring out and put it down in front of Cherry. "Here's a little gift for you," I said.

She examined the stone. "Why, it looks real!"

"It is."

"Are you so rich, Ray?"

"No. It took a slice of my savings to pay for it."

She slipped the ring on her finger. "She refused to take it — is that it?"

"She took it all right," I said. "We were engaged a couple of months ago. Last night she gave it back to me."

"Another man, Ray?"

"A doctor who has a flourishing

practice on Eastern Parkway. I suppose she prefers being a doctor's wife to —" I scowled in my beer. "I should be fair to her. She said she found out she loves him and doesn't love me. It happens. I believe her. So what?" I drank my beer.

Cherry turned her hand this way and that so the diamond would catch the light. Last night, after I had left Florence's house, I had come close to throwing the ring down the sewer. I'd done something like that now by giving it to her. Let twelve hundred dollars go down the drain along with the woman I loved.

She leaned toward me across the table. "Honey, would you like to go somewhere with me for a few days?"

"You don't have to pay for it," I growled.

"It's not because of the ring. It's you I want. I've fallen for you, Ray — that manly build of yours and your sweet ways. Take back the ring and I'll still want to go with you. We'll pick up my bag at my hotel and stop off at your place for some of your clothes and we'll drive in your car to Vermont or New Hampshire, somewhere up north, and have one swell time."

"Wait a minute. You mean leave today?"

"Why not? We'll drive till dark and stop off at a tourist cabin for the night and go on in the morning."

I shook my head. "I've got to be at work tomorrow."

"But you said the business is yours — yours and your father's. You can get off for a few days."

I could, but I didn't tell her that. I said, "We've tonight ahead of us and we can keep seeing each other during the week."

"Either we leave right now or it's nothing." Her hand dropped on mine. Her over-painted lips were slightly parted and her eyes glowed with promise. "Let's make a real thing of it, honey. You can get away if you want to."

"It's impossible," I lied.

She sat back, pouting. "That means you don't want to."

I didn't know whether I did or didn't. I'd already done one damn fool thing by giving her the ring. I didn't regret it, but I had a feeling I'd very much regret shacking up with her for a few days, becoming involved with her. Maybe she scared me by moving so fast. Why so much, so quickly? All I wanted was a few hours of diversion, to get back on balance if I could after the blow Florence had given me.

What did she really want? I found it hard to believe that all she was after was me.

I muttered, "I'm sorry, Cherry," and finished what was left in my glass.

She stood up and strode out to the street.

So that was that. She was gone and the ring with her. I didn't mind about the ring. What was the difference which sewer I had thrown it down? I minded her walking out on me more, but not so much that

I couldn't pass it off with a shrug. Probably it was for the best. There was something queer about her. I paid the check and went out.

She was waiting for me at the edge of a crowd listening to a freak show barker.

She had a smile for me. "I'll get dressed and then you can buy me a dinner," she said as if nothing had happened.

That was the way I preferred it. A date for the evening. No strings. No complications.

Her hotel was between Mermaid and Neptune Avenues. It was a square, two-story wooden structure, and like most small Coney Island hotels it looked as if nobody ever went in or out of it.

The dusty little foyer was empty. We walked up a flight of dim stairs and she unlocked a door and I followed her into a room that held a bed and a chair and a dresser and a bit of extra space.

"Don't lift your arms or you'll knock something over," she said. "The bathroom's in the hall. I'll be back in a minute, honey."

I sat down on the chair. The Sunday paper was scattered on the bed. I hadn't read the paper this morning because I'd been too upset over my experience with Florence to keep my mind on anything. Waiting for Cherry, I picked up the news section of the Sunday *Courier* and found it folded to the story of the armored car holdup on an inside page.

Only half a column was devoted to it now, two days later, because the police hadn't gotten anywhere at all. There was one clue, if it could be called that. A witness at a window had seen one of the bandits, just before jumping into the getaway car, stop to talk to a woman parked in a snappy convertible. Probably he had merely warned her not to scream, but she and her car had disappeared almost at once and that made the police curious. They were looking for her; they had nobody else to look for. About all the woman at the window had seen of her had been her hair, and that had been bright red. The convertible had also been red — a combination easy to remember.

I turned the page. Cherry came back.

I had expected her to change to street clothes in the bathroom, considering the lack of privacy in that tiny room, but she was still wearing her yellow bathing suit. She gave me a vague kind of smile, and without turning her back she opened a zipper and pushed down the top of her suit. Her breasts jumped out. They were firm and high.

She just stood there and let me look at her. No, there was nothing subtle about Cherry Drew.

I rose from the chair. I put my hands on her.

"Will you take me up north tonight?" she demanded, holding my wrists.

So this display of her body was a

come-on. Yet the set-up was all screwy. If she was so much on the make, the ring I had given her should have been quite a haul, better than she could have hoped from the likes of me. But it hadn't seemed to mean much to her; the only thing that did was getting me to go off with her.

"Let's discuss that later," I said. "Meanwhile . . ."

She twisted her mouth away from my kiss. "Damn you, Ray! Take me away from here or get the hell out! For God's sake, take me away!"

It was as if something had cracked in her, letting pent-up hysteria trickle through. Her fingernails were dug into my arms and she was shaking me. Suddenly I saw her as a frightened and lonely girl who needed me the way nobody ever had before. Certainly more than Florence ever had.

I pulled her to me and she felt small and helpless against my chest. "Take it easy, Cherry," I said stroking her red hair.

She clung to me, muttering, "Honey, we can have such a time together. Just us two in a little bungalow up in the hills. I won't hold you to anything. You can leave any time you feel like. I'll be so good to you."

It sounded fine. Maybe like myself she was on a rebound from love and needed to have the emptiness filled.

I said, "All right, Cherry."

She sighed and let herself go in my arms. But after a minute she pulled away from me. "We've got to hurry, honey."

"That's what I don't understand — why the rush?"

She had stepped to the clothes closet at the rear of the room. She paused with her hand on the knob, and I knew that she was fishing for an answer that would sound reasonable, at least more or less.

The answer never came because, after all, she hadn't hurried enough. The other door started to open — the one from the hall.

It opened very quietly. A man stepped in with a gun in his hand.

He was squat and his blue automatic was squat and half his wide face consisted of a squashed nose. His left hand reached behind him and closed the door.

"Pardon me for barging in like this," he said drily.

Her lover or her husband, I thought, and he held that gun as if he meant to use it.

Cherry was staring at him over one bare shoulder. She did nothing about the top half of her bathing suit dangling from her waist, and I could see the slight stirring of her naked breasts. That was the only sign of emotion — of anything. She uttered no sound.

The silence held for no more than a long moment, but it built up unendurable tension. I towered over both of them. I felt as if I were filling most of that small room, making too big a target. There would hardly be space for me to fall when he shot me.

I said, "Wait a minute. Let me explain."

The squat man looked me up and down. Then he looked at Cherry and said, "Who's the guy?"

"Nobody. A pickup." Her voice was husky and less controlled than her face.

"Then what's he want to explain?"

"I guess he thinks you're my boy friend," she said, and only now she was slowly and indifferently pulling up her yellow bathing suit.

He chuckled. "As if I give a damn who you mess with. And you don't have to worry Georgie will ever give a damn."

A shiver ran through her. "What did you do to him?"

"What d'you think? Walt's smart. When you didn't show pretty soon after we got there, Walt got leery. He had some of the boys keep an eye on Georgie and they nabbed him trying to sneak away." He grinned hideously. "The Barber got out his matches and made him talk. That's how come we knew you was here in Coney."

"So Georgie is dead," she whispered.

It wasn't a question and he didn't have to answer it. In the world in which they lived there was a certain cause and effect. Georgie had done something and had been tortured until he revealed information and then he had been killed.

"Where is it?" the squat man demanded.

Cherry straightened her shoulders, and whatever she felt about the death of Georgie no longer showed. "It's in the car, Shorty."

"Where's it parked?"

"A few blocks away."

"Don't kid me. The papers say your red heap's hot. It was spotted by somebody, and your red hair too. You'd ditch the heap, that's what you'd do."

I got it then. I blurted, "So you two — in that holdup!"

That seemed to remind Shorty I was in the room. He pointed his gun more toward me than toward her. "So this is just a punk, eh?"

"You talked too much, Shorty," she said. "The papers are full of it."

He shrugged. "What's the difference? Your friend just stepped in over his head. Open that closet door, Cherry."

She didn't move. She said, "Shorty, we'll make a deal."

"Huh! Think I'm as dumb as you and Georgie? I'll take just my cut and keep on living."

"Shorty, listen!"

He patted the gun barrel. "Baby, you do the listening when I have the heater."

She obeyed. She pulled the closet door open and sidled against the wall and stood with her back against the dresser. She hadn't said a word to me, hadn't even looked at me. Neither had Shorty addressed me. I wasn't worth it. I was a punk.

All of a sudden I was more angry than anything else.

Shorty glanced into the closet. He grunted. "Two big bags. Big enough to hold it." He waved the gun at me. "Punk, lug them two bags out and open them. I gotta make sure what's in 'em."

He stepped aside to let me get by. The room was so small that what with the furniture he couldn't put more than a couple of feet distance between us. When I passed him, I used a little trick I had learned fighting in a war against a lot tougher killers than Shorty. My left forearm slammed down on his gunwrist and with the same motion I twisted my torso and smashed my right fist into his jaw.

I might be a punk, but when I hit the hard guys they felt it.

He might have gone all the way down if the corner of the dresser hadn't stopped him. He bounced back and tottered toward the bed. The gun was still in his hand, but he wasn't doing anything with it. I couldn't be sure I'd paralyzed the nerve. With both hands I grabbed at the wrist that held the gun, and he uttered a gushing sigh and toppled forward against me. And behind him was Cherry and something was flashing in her hand.

She leaned forward against him, and over his shoulder our eyes met. There seemed to be a fever in hers. She pulled back, drawing out the knife, and he kept sinking. Then he pitched forward; his head struck the bed and he flopped over on his side.

Cherry slumped back against the dresser and stared at the red wetness on the blade of the long, slender knife in her hand. She had stabbed him twice.

Shorty was dead, all right. He had no pulse. Crouching over him, I could see the two small holes ringed with red in the back of his white shirt. There had been little bleeding because death had come quickly. One of the thrusts must have hit a vulnerable spot, probably the tip of the blade going far enough into his back to touch his heart.

The silence held. There were not even street sounds. It was too hot. People hadn't yet come back from the beach or were taking it easy in the shade.

I looked up at Cherry. The top of her bathing suit was again dangling from her waist; she hadn't taken the time or trouble to secure it. She was wiping the blade on a handful of face tissues.

The most shocking thing of all that had happened was her calmness.

"Doesn't it even bother you?" I said.

"He would've killed us both. Didn't you know that?"

"I had him. He was half out on his feet and I was taking his gun from him."

"How could I tell? His back was to me. I figured in a moment he'd plug you and then me."

There was a click and the blade

snapped out of sight into the handle of the knife. It was a killer's weapon.

"Where did you have it?" I asked her.

"Under that blouse on the dresser. I grabbed it when you socked him." She skirted the legs of the dead man on the way to the foot of the bed and wrapped the bloody tissues in a sheet of newspaper. "You sure were right, honey, when you said you could take care of yourself. I don't know anybody who could have taken him better."

"Not even Georgie?"

A shadow crossed her face — almost a child's face with that button nose and cute turned-up chin and clear eyes. Not the face, looking at it, of a girl who had just killed a man and then had calmly wiped the blood off the knife.

I started toward the door.

"Where are you going, Ray?" she said sharply.

"Out of here, of course."

"To the cops?"

"I don't know," I said. Without taking my hand from the doorknob I turned to her.

She had picked up Shorty's gun. She wasn't pointing it at me. She just held it by the trigger guard.

"The law will say you had as much to do with killing him as I did," she told me. "You want us both to burn in the chair?"

"It was self-defense."

"You heard what's in the closet. How'll you explain that?"

"I'll tell the truth."

She laughed mirthlessly. "Try to make the cops believe you and me weren't out to get away with it when Shorty walked in to stop us. And I'll swear you were in it with me all along. By God, I will!"

I didn't doubt her. "All right," I said, "I'll keep my mouth shut."

I turned the doorknob.

"Ray, you can't leave me flat like this. I need you. Everybody's after me — the cops and Shorty's pals."

I hesitated. "You think the gang has surrounded the hotel?"

"I wouldn't be standing here talking if I thought so. They didn't find out from Georgie where I was staying. I didn't know myself where I'd stay till I got here Friday. He was supposed to meet me as soon as he could near the jetty on Bay 19. I guess they headed straight there, but we'd already left. Then they scattered to look for me."

"How do you know all this?"

"It figures. Shorty spotted me when I was walking along with you. He tailed us."

"Then he went and phoned the others," I put in.

"No. Let me tell you. I know more about how they'd operate. At this minute the rest of them are out looking for me. They have no headquarters in Coney Island except maybe a car parked in a certain place — no phone where he could call them. Because look — would Shorty have come in here alone if he didn't have to? He saw you, a husky guy, with me. At least two men were needed, one to take care of us and one to handle the stuff. More would've been better. But Shorty was afraid if he left to get help, we might be gone before he could return with them. I think he listened at the door and heard us say we were leaving right away. So he had to make his move then and there."

I was listening to all that with only half a mind, my thoughts jumping about, and suddenly the whole thing became ridiculous, me lingering at the door, listening to this half-naked girl who was twirling a heavy gun on her finger and talking quietly and reasonably and objectively while the body of the man she had killed a very few minutes ago lay huddled behind her on the floor.

I said bitterly, "What do you need me for then — to help you carry out the eighty thousand dollars?"

"Yes, honey. Our eighty grand. Yours and mine."

I just stood there.

Cherry came over. She reached around me and snapped the lock shut. "In case anybody does try to come in," she explained. "Should've locked it before." Done with that piece of business, she pressed herself against me.

"Georgie's dead, so you need me," I said tonelessly.

"Don't always argue so much." Her hips stirred. "Eighty grand, honey. Mostly small bills. They can never be traced. Vermont or New Hampshire, like I said. A bungalow in the hills. Later Europe. We can live like kings."

I didn't say yes, but neither did I say no.

I don't know if I thought of the money, at least consciously, or if at the moment I was very much aware of her body imposing itself on me. It was as if I were drifting without moving from the spot, letting whatever currents there were take me and not particularly caring where. It occurred to me that Florence had a great deal to do with the way I was reacting. But then, so did Cherry.

I said, "I suppose if they catch up to you they'll kill you."

"Yes. Like they killed Georgie. I can't get away from them without you and your car."

"And from the police," I muttered.

"You see, honey, how I'm boxed in."

She was, but only as long as she clung to the loot. She could manage to slip away by bus or train, but what she'd needed me for from the first was to transport eighty thousand dollars in cash. I didn't mention that.

"Well," I said, "I can't let them kill you."

I had to straighten the legs of the dead man before I could shove him under the bed.

That part bothered me the least; I had seen too many dead men in the war. I had eaten and slept surrounded by them, and some had been my buddies. The mere physical presence of death, especially now that the body was out of sight, bothered me least of all. And neither did it seem to bother Cherry.

The consequences of his death were something else.

"The police will get a description of you from the others in the hotel," I said.

She was wiggling out of her yellow bathing suit. "Shorty won't be found till tomorrow when the chambermaid cleans the room. Of course I gave a phony name. We'll drive all night, so by that time we'll be hundreds of miles away. I'll change the color of my hair soon as I have time. And you don't have to worry about yourself. Nobody saw you come in with me."

She left the bathing suit on the floor and moved to the dresser. Her body was very beautiful. Almost, I reached for her. The only thing that stopped me was the dead man under the bed. I sat tight in the chair and tried not to look at her.

The closet door remained open. Only one dress hung there. The rest of it was filled by two very large suitcases and a plastic weekend bag sitting on top of them. The small bag would hold all her clothes. There wouldn't be room for anything but the money in the suitcases.

I said, "It was clever. You were parked near where the holdup took place. As they ran by, they tossed the money into your convertible. You drove calmly away. A pretty girl in a snappy convertible wouldn't be stopped by the police or suspected. And if the men were picked up while trying to make their getaway, the evidence wouldn't be found on them."

Shrugging, she took underwear out of the top drawer of her dresser.

"But you and Georgie planned to doublecross them," I said. "No honor among thieves."

Cherry swung around to me. "There were seven of them besides me. Walt was going to get the big share because he was the brains. Not such a fortune would be left after the rest was split. Anyway, they were only going to toss me a few grand — less than anybody else because I was a woman." Her red mouth got a hard, ugly twist to it. "All my life I've been poor. How long would two-three grand last me? Then I'd be back grubbing for every cent. Hustling for it. Yeah, hustling. I wanted a chance, and this was it."

And she had talked Georgie into the doublecross, I thought. She must have had her clothes off at the time and he had given in and now he was dead.

"But it went wrong," I said. "He was supposed to meet you at the jetty next day — yesterday. Coney Island would be a good place; you can get lost in the crowds. But he didn't show up, and this morning you read in the paper that the police were looking for a red-headed girl in a red convertible. They'd be watching the road; the car became a menace. You got rid of it, left it somewhere on a street. You brought the suitcases up here, one at a time, needing all your strength to lug them, because that much cash would have plenty of weight. Then you went back to the beach. Georgie still didn't show. You began to realize that he had been made to talk. When I called your name, you nearly jumped out of your skin because you thought it was one of them. It turned out to be only me, Ray Whitehead, and for a minute you wanted no part of me. Then it struck you that maybe here was a sucker you could use to move the money for you."

She had everything on but her dress. "But after a little while I went for you, honey. I really did. I haven't known many sweet guys like you." With nylon-encased hips swinging, she came to where I sat and stood against my knees. "I've fallen for you. We can make a good thing out of it. And we're rich."

I kept my hands from her. I said, without looking at her, "I'll drive you, but that's all. I don't want any part of the stolen money. I'll take you wherever you want and then go home."

She didn't argue. She smiled a little, as if she knew better. She turned from me and took the print dress from the closet and dropped it over her head.

"Bring your car around," she said. "But not too near. There's a back way out to the showers and an alley to the other street. While you're gone I'll wipe our prints off everything."

"Mightn't it be better to wait until dark? We can be sure they don't know you're at this hotel or they would have been here already."

"I can't stand waiting." She nodded toward the bed. "Especially with that in the room."

I had an idea that what bothered her a lot more than the dead man was the possibility that I'd change my mind if we hung around in that room too long.

"All right," I said.

I unlocked the door and opened it a crack and listened. The hall was silent. The hotel retained that feeling of being deserted. I didn't see anybody until I was out the back door and then there were only a couple of small children squealing under the open shower in the yard. I crossed over to the alley on the other side of the yard and went up it to the street.

My car was in a parking lot half a dozen blocks away. Walking there, I thought a great deal of her and the money. I wasn't arguing with myself. I kept seeing how she had looked when she had stepped out of the yellow bathing suit, and through my mind flitted plans of where we could go and what we could do with eighty thousand dollars in cash.

It wasn't until some minutes later, when I had rolled my car out of the parking lot, that I remembered I'd told her I wanted no part of her or the money after I'd driven her to safety. She hadn't believed me, and maybe I hadn't believed myself but had mouthed noble sentiments to kid myself. Well, it was time I stopped kidding myself. I'd tried the respectable way with Florence, and she had thrown the ring back at me because I wasn't a doctor. The ring now was Cherry's, and that could be a symbol. My future had become tied up with Cherry Drew.

I parked my car a hundred feet from the mouth of the alley. In the hotel lobby I met two middle-aged women. They were so busy gabbing they didn't as much as glance at me.

I found Cherry wiping her fingerprints from the dresser mirror.

"Everything all right?" she asked.

"What could go wrong at this point?"

"Nothing, I guess."

As a trucker, I was used to handling heavy packages. I had thought I could take down both suitcases at once, but when I pulled one out of the closet and lifted it I learned how heavy tightly-packed money could be, if there was enough of it. Halfway to my car the suitcase began to strain my muscles and I had to use both hands on the handle. I couldn't understand how she had managed to get it up to her room. I locked it in the trunk of my car and went back for the other one.

Cherry was snapping her little weekend bag closed.

"We mustn't be seen leaving together," she said. "I'll wait a few minutes after you're gone and leave the front way."

"Will you have to check out?"

"I paid in advance through today. This place is run more like a rooming house than a hotel." She took a huge straw handbag from the dresser and hung it over her shoulder. "Park as close as you can on Mermaid Avenue, on this side of the street toward Sea Gate. I'll come walking by. Keep an eye peeled for me because I don't know your car."

I pulled the second suitcase out of the closet. When I turned, I could see from there the soles of one of Shorty's shoes.

"What happened to his gun?" I asked her.

She tapped her handbag. "In here. Why, do you want it?"

"No." I looked at her standing so trim and pretty in that gay print dress. I said, "I suppose you realize I can drive off with the money without waiting for you."

"You could, but you wouldn't."

"Don't tell me you trust anybody?"

"You're not anybody, honey." She rose on her toes and held my face between her hands and kissed me hard on the mouth. "It's you and me from now on. Nothing will break us up."

For a little while I held her. Then I said, "I'll be waiting in my car," and took the second suitcase out of the room.

For eight minutes by my watch I sat in my car on Mermaid Avenue, a block and a half from the front entrance of the hotel. Add to that the time it had taken me to carry the suitcase to my car and lock it in the trunk along with the other one and drive here and manoeuver into the only parking space on the street, and close to fifteen minutes had passed since I had left her.

Had anything gone wrong?

There would have been no point to her leaving more than five minutes after I had. But say it was ten minutes — it would take her only two more at the most to walk this far. I sat twisted around on the seat, staring up the street.

The second hand of my watch swept around twice more. Then I couldn't stand it any longer. I started up the car and drove around the block to the hotel.

Two women stood talking at the entrance — the two I had met in the lobby when returning from my trip with the first suitcase. They'd been at it a good half-hour or more. I stopped my car smack in the middle of the street while trying to decide to pull over and go up to the room and see if she was still there.

Behind me a horn honked. I gave a taxi room to slip by and rolled slowly on. Maybe she was ahead of me, looking for me on Mermaid Avenue.

She was ahead of me, all right, but not walking. She stood against the window of an empty store near the corner, and two men were with her.

One was burly and had jowls. The other was gaunt and completely bald. They wore conservative business suits and regular shirts and neckties in a locality where almost everybody went in for light or sport clothes, especially during a hot day.

They would be either detectives or two of the gangsters.

My first impulse was to keep going. But at the moment I had no reason to fear either cops or gangsters; they couldn't know me or what was in my car. I paused where I was, no more than thirty feet from them on my left.

The burly man had her straw handbag and was looking in it. The bald man held her arm with his left hand and his right hand was sunk deep in his pocket.

I knew then that they weren't cops, because the burly man didn't take out Shorty's automatic. A cop would have. He kept rummaging around.

I had no doubt that the one who was holding her by the arm had a gun in his pocket.

She lifted her head and saw me. Within minutes her face had aged. There were lines about her eyes and mouth and her eyes had dulled with hopelessness.

Her lips moved soundlessly, spreading, forming the same unspoken syllable again and again. "Go," she was telling me. "Go . . . go . . ."

I didn't know what to do. If I had taken Shorty's automatic, I could stroll casually up to them and have them covered before they could pull their own guns out. But she had it and it could do her no good.

Suddenly she spoke up loudly. "Walt," she said to the burly man, "you got a bum steer from Georgie."

She was letting me know who they were in case I wasn't sure. Walt — that was the name she and Shorty had mentioned as belonging to the leader of the gang.

Scowling, the bald man glanced around. I dipped my head over the wheel and raced my engine, making like a driver who was having trouble with his car. Nobody else was near just then. He squeezed her arm and whispered something to her. Her body drooped.

The other man, Walt, took a piece of paper out of her handbag and read it.

A horn reminded me that I was again blocking traffic. I rolled the car to clear space at a fire hydrant across the street from Cherry and the gangsters. I pulled up the handbrake and looked to the left and they were no longer in front of the store window.

They were walking up the street, Cherry in the middle. From my car I watched them enter the hotel.

Walt must have come across the hotel receipt in her handbag. They would take her up to her room and find Shorty's body under the bed. But they wouldn't find the money. She had urged me to go. It was too late for her; there was nothing I could do for her. Go, she had said in effect, and save yourself.

I drove around the corner. The space on Mermaid Avenue where I had been parked a few minutes ago to wait for her was still empty. I rolled a little way past it and stopped and realized I couldn't run out on her just like that. At least, I needed time to think. I backed in against the curb and cut the engine and lit a cigarette.

There must have been method in their luck at coming up that street just after she left the hotel. Walt was smart, Shorty had said. He would have to be to pull off an armored car holdup without a hitch — anyway, no hitch at the time. The organizer type of criminal, planning each detail to the split-second. In the same way he would have organized the hunt for Cherry. When she hadn't been found at either of the jetties in Bay 19, he'd divided narrow Coney Island into sections and detailed a man to patrol each section and report back to a central place every so often. Shorty's failure to report back had made Walt concentrate his forces on this particular section. It would have been only a hunch that Shorty had found something, but a calculated hunch.

Something like that. Because however they worked, it would be in a highly organized fashion, like an army patrol, where each man knew exactly what he was about. How could you fight that kind of setup if you were on the wrong side of the law too, and couldn't go anywhere for help?

I couldn't abandon her to them. They would do to her what they had done to Georgie, torture her and then kill her.

She would be better off in the hands of the police. Better to spend years of her life in jail.

But what about me? I'd go to jail too.

Leave her. She was no better than they. In some ways worse because she had doublecrossed them.

What about the money?

I didn't want one cursed cent of it. Not without her. She'd guessed that; she'd known I wouldn't take it unless she went with it. Tonight I'd dump the two suitcases in an empty lot.

I pressed the starter. I listened to the engine idle and suddenly I cut the switch and pulled out the key. I'd make a deal with them. The money in return for her life.

I locked the car doors and walked toward the hotel.

They were coming out of the hotel when I approached it. They turned as one, as soldiers on parade, Cherry still between them, and when they had taken several steps toward me she saw me approach.

She stopped and they stopped. She said something and pointed at me. The bald man hurried forward with his right hand in his pocket.

"This is a rod," he said, pressing against my side so I could feel the muzzle poke me through the material. "Get over to the wall. Act like nothing's wrong or I'll plug you."

I stepped over to the brick side of an apartment building. A woman passed, wheeling a baby carriage. More people were now on the street. The afternoon was wearing on; they were coming from the beach. There could be no help from any of them.

Walt and Cherry came up to us. His arm was through hers, as if in intimacy; nobody seeing them would guess they weren't on the best of terms. He also had his right hand in his pocket, carelessly, jauntily, but his finger was around a trigger.

I said, "Listen, I'll—"

"You do the listening," Walt cut me off. "Take us to your car."

I looked at Cherry. She dropped her eyes.

"It'll have to be a deal," I said, "The money is all yours if you let us alone."

"Sure thing," Walt smiled; it wasn't a nice smile. "Like I told Cherry, the dough's all we're after."

The bald man and I led the way. He walked on my left, his pocketed gun inches from my ribs. I thought I might have a chance to take him, the way I had Shorty, but not with Cherry and Walt and his own gun ten feet behind.

We crossed the street and turned right on Mermaid. And suddenly I knew that I was taking both myself and Cherry to our deaths.

They couldn't afford to do it any other way. There was a murdered man in the room Cherry had occupied and if she was picked up there was a good chance she would talk. I, whom they knew nothing about, might be even more dangerous to them as far as the police were concerned.

Three people had already died because of the holdup — the armored car guard and Georgie and Shorty. Why not two more? When we reached my car and I gave them the keys, they would make us get in and drive away with them. Wherever they took us, we'd never come back.

I walked past my car without glancing at it. We went a block and a half more, and the bald man was beginning to growl about the distance, when I saw a cop.

They say there's never a cop when you need one. But if you walk far enough you'll meet one. He was strolling toward us, looking bored.

The bald man whispered, "Don't try anything."

I sure was going to. I sang out, "Officer, can you tell me where the subway station is?"

The cop sauntered over. "You're going the wrong way."

I turned. Walt and Cherry had also stopped. "He says we're going the wrong way."

"Is that so?" Cherry slipped her arm out of Walt's and moved to my side and took my arm instead. "Is it far, officer?"

He suggested that we take the bus. Cherry said she didn't mind walking. And Walt and the bald man stood by, trying not to show what they felt.

Then we were moving away from them, walking with the cop. Cherry managed to keep him with us by carrying on an animated conversation about this being our first trip to Coney Island and how excited we were. I glanced back. Walt and the bald man were tagging after us at a short distance.

At the corner we lost the cop. That turned out to be the end of his beat. The two men came at us, not quite running, but closing the distance fast.

Ahead was my car, but we couldn't hope to get to it and unlock a door and drive off before they were on us. On the right, across the street and a block away, was Surf Avenue with its rides and sideshows and crowds. We could lose ourselves there among the thousands.

"This way," I said, grabbing her hand.

A bus charged down on us when we were halfway across the street — a break because we could duck behind it, putting it between us and the gangsters. When we made the opposite sidewalk, I glanced back. We were due for some little luck; we got it in a sudden stream of cars going in both directions, and they were still on the other side. We ran toward Surf Avenue.

There were quite a few people on

this street. They impeded us, and what made it harder still was that we wouldn't let go of each other's hands.

She gasped, "Are they coming?"

"I don't see them."

Surf Avenue, when we reached it, was a disappointment. Always before it had seemed jammed. Maybe it was too early and people were lingering on the beach and boardwalk. Anyway, there weren't enough for us.

We were in front of a shooting gallery that had no customers. Next door was a roller coaster. A car was about to leave and there was no line waiting to get on. As good a place as any to hide within moments.

I handed the ticket agent a dollar and snatched the two tickets from her hand without waiting for the thirty cents change. We leaped into the roller coaster car a moment before it started. We sat low in the seat, holding onto each other.

"Oh, God, Ray," she whispered, "I couldn't help telling them. They said they'd let the Barber work on me. You don't know what he does to people. I had to tell them it was in your car."

"I don't blame you. Forget it."

We were crawling up the first incline. I looked down. The people below were just people — nobody who could be recognized. I braced my feet against the footboard.

She screamed and clung frantically to me when we went down. The car leveled off for a moment and she recovered her breath and moaned, "How I've always hated these things!" I laughed brokenly and held her close as we went down another dip and swung sickeningly around a curve.

They were there when we reached the end of the ride, the burly gang leader and the bald man standing beside the ticket booth. Both had their hands in their pockets.

Cherry spotted them first, when the car was rolling to a stop. She whispered, "They saw us getting on. They'll stay there till we get off, and pretty soon the others will join them."

"Then we'll stay on," I said.

A man moved along the car collecting the fares of those who were after more of the same. I paid him and put my arm back around Cherry.

"What good will it do?" she said. "We can't ride on here forever."

I hadn't anything to say. Again we were crawling up that long, steep incline. It was quiet up there. I could clearly hear the barking of rifles in the shooting gallery next door to the roller coaster.

She screamed and dug into me as we followed our stomachs down. After a minute, when it wasn't so bad, I said, "I think you really care for me."

"I do, Ray. More than anything."

"Listen. When we get off and I start shooting, run. Don't stop for anything."

"But you haven't a . . . a . . ."

"Yes, I have," I said.

There were three of them when we got off the roller coaster. I hardly looked at the newcomer. They closed in on us.

I stepped away from Cherry. Walt stuck to my side. He said, "Got wise to yourself, eh?" and I said, "Yes," and on my right was the sign reading, "10 SHOTS FOR 25¢." Only one man was shooting at the far end of the counter.

I slammed my shoulder against Walt and lunged past him. I snatched up a rifle. It was fastened to the counter by a thin chain, but there was enough play to let me turn with it. Both Walt and the bald man were digging their guns out of their pockets.

I shot one and then the other in almost the same instant. The rifle was only a .22, but at that range effective enough.

I didn't see the third gangster. I didn't see Cherry either. In front of me the street had cleared of people. But somebody was grabbing me from behind. I gave up the gun and didn't struggle against the two husky men who held me.

Both men lay on the sidewalk. The bald man was writhing. Walt was motionless except for a twitching arm. I didn't care whether they lived or died.

The police arrived, a horde of them. The crowd returned and formed a gawking semi-circle around the shooting gallery.

And I was saying to a uniformed sergeant, "These two are part of the gang that held up the armored car Friday. They've got guns. They tried to kill me. The eighty thousand dollars are in my car on Mermaid Avenue."

"So you're one of 'em!"

"No, Sergeant. It's a long story. I don't know if anybody will believe me."

Cherry said, "They'll believe you. You had nothing to do with it. You didn't know what was in the suitcases till just now. I'll swear you didn't."

She had come back. She had pushed her way through the crowd and was standing trim in that print dress and her flaming hair was loose about her shoulders. And as she spoke to the sergeant, she kept twisting on her finger the ring I had given her.

I was sorry she hadn't kept going.

Kid Stuff

Dad had called it kid stuff, but I wasn't a kid any longer. I was man enough to kill . . .

HE SAT VERY STILL on the side of his bed, running the ball of his thumb slowly along the edge of the hunting knife. From the bathroom at the end of the hall he could hear the soft whir of his father's electric razor.

It was funny, he thought, how every tiny, ordinary sound seemed louder tonight; louder, and somehow important. And it was strange, too, that he felt so calm. Until this afternoon, his mind had been a vortex of fear and jealousy and hate; and then something deep inside him had seemed to burst, and he had realized with numbing suddenness that he was going to kill a man he had never met.

He was going to take the hunting knife and kill the man who had stolen Laurie Jackson away from him.

BY

JONATHAN CRAIG

The agony and frustrated helplessness had left him, abruptly and completely, and he'd found he could think of Laurie in very nearly an emotional vacuum. It was almost as if he had now become someone else; an onlooker, interested but emotionless.

There was a soft knock at the door, and suddenly he became aware that the whirring of his father's razor in the bathroom had stopped.

He quickly slipped the knife into the waistband of his slacks and pulled his loose-fitting sport shirt down over it.

"Come on in," he said.

His father came into the room, a thin, slightly stooped man grown gray at the temples. There were tired lines at the corners of his eyes and around his mouth as he nodded to Chris and came over to sit on the side of the bed.

"You still want to borrow the car tonight, Chris?" he asked.

"Not if you'd rather drive it to your lodge meeting," Chris said.

His father grinned wryly. "No. A salesman gets enough driving on his job. And besides, I've been feeling a little seedy lately. A long walk would probably do me a lot of good." He cleared his throat, and Chris could sense the uncertainty and embarrassment his father must be feeling. His father hadn't come to talk about the car; he knew. The poor guy, he thought; he hates this.

"Uh, Chris . . ." his father said.

Chris stared hard at the far wall, trying not to let his eyes stray to Laurie's picture on the dresser. "Yes, Dad?"

"I — uh — well, I thought maybe it'd be a good idea if you and I sort of had a little talk."

"About Laurie, you mean?" Chris asked.

"Yes. About Laurie." His father leaned forward, elbows on knees, not looking at Chris. "I've been pretty concerned about you lately. You've been depressed, and you haven't been eating properly, and more than once you've passed me in the house without even knowing I was there." He glanced at Chris, then away again. "It's something we all have to go through, I guess. People kid a lot about it, but puppy love can be mighty painful."

Chris moistened his lips. "Puppy love, Dad?"

"Doesn't seem that way to you, does it, son? Seems like the world's come to an end. Sure. I know how it is. It's rough." He took a deep breath. "It can be the worst kind of sickness there is."

The blade of the hunting knife was cold against Chris' stomach. He moistened his lips again.

"I think it would be best if you forgot about her, son," his father said. "I know it would hurt, but later on . . ." He shrugged. "You know a lot for a seventeen-year-old, Chris, but a boy your age can't be expected to have too much . . . well, perspective."

"Maybe so," Chris said. He's a

good guy, he thought. The best dad a guy ever had. But ever since Mother died, he's been a little confused. He tries to do everything the way he thinks she'd do it if she were still here. He wants to help me, but he doesn't know what the hell to do.

"Yes, Dad," he said gently. "I guess you're right."

His father got up and walked to the dresser and stood looking at Laurie's photograph.

"Dark eyes and blonde hair," he said. "An unusual combination, Chris. And very, very pretty."

Chris didn't say anything.

His father came back to the bed and sat down again. "But she's only seventeen, too," he said. "Too young to know her own mind yet — just like you, Chris." He took a cigarette from his pocket and lighted it and blew smoke toward the floor. "I have a little confession to make, son . . ."

The poor guy, Chris thought; the poor guy. "What is it?" he asked.

"I went down to this diner where Laurie works, to look her over." He shrugged apologetically. "You know how it is, son. I was worried about you, and all, and — well, I felt I had to know what kind of girl she was. I should have mentioned it sooner, I know, but I thought things might work out of their own accord."

"You talked to her?" Chris asked.

"No. But I spent about an hour at the counter there, watching her, listening to her talk to people. You know."

If there was only something I could say to him, Chris thought. Anything at all. The guy's giving himself a bad time — and all for nothing. It must have been worrying him plenty lately, the way he looks, so tired and half sick all the time. "What'd you think of her?" he asked.

"Like I said, she's very pretty."

Chris laughed shortly, thinking of how abruptly Laurie had thrown him over for this other guy. The other guy, she'd said, was handsome, and what's more he was a guy who knew the score. Chris, she'd said, was still a baby. The other guy knew more about women than Chris would ever know. A real, honest-to-God *man*, she'd said.

He put his hand down firmly on his father's leg and smiled at him. "Don't worry about it, Dad. I know she's not for me."

His father looked at him searchingly. "You're sure?"

"Positive. Like you said, it's just something we all have to go through."

"I hope so," his father said. "From what I saw and overheard at the diner, I'd say Laurie's pretty mature for her age. A girl of seventeen is a different proposition from a boy the same age, you know. I got the impression . . ." He spread his hands helplessly. "Well, you know what I mean."

Chris thought of the first date he'd had with Laurie, of the way she'd suddenly become the aggressor, insistent and insatiable. He remembered the feel of her sharp little teeth in his shoulder and the burn of her fingernails as they raked his naked back.

"I hate to say anything against someone you're fond of," his father said, "but —"

"Sure," Chris said. "Forget it." He let his smile widen.

His father studied him. "I can start thinking of you as normal again, eh, Chris?"

"Sure thing, Dad."

His father rose and walked toward the door. "There's lots of girls, Chris — and lots of time." He reached into his pocket and tossed a key folder to the bed. "There's your keys. Have a good time tonight, fella." His voice, beneath its tone of friendly banter, was relieved, more assured. He grinned and his slumped shoulders straightened a little. "Don't knock off any fenders."

"I won't," Chris said. He watched the door close behind his father. The poor guy, he thought again.

He glanced at his watch. Five minutes past seven. That left almost an hour to kill before Laurie got off work at eight. He felt restless, now that he'd talked with his father, and the room seemed to be closing in about him. He got to his feet, raked loose change and house key from the top of his dresser, glanced once at Laurie's dark-eyed loveliness, and went down the back stairs to the garage.

He drove aimlessly, following streets where traffic was lightest, thinking of his father and of how little his father really knew about him. He was still a child to him, a runny-nosed kid with scabs on his knees. His father was even worse than his mother had been. Puppy love! he thought. My God! He ran the tips of his fingers lightly along the outline of the knife beneath his shirt. Puppy love!

The long minutes dragged by somehow, and at eight o'clock he parked the car half a block from the diner where Laurie worked and turned off the lights. If the new guy picked her up after work, fine; he'd follow them, and after the guy took Laurie home, he'd follow *him* until he had a chance to use the knife. If the guy didn't show up, then there'd always be another night. The knife would be just as sharp then as it was now — and the other guy's death just as sure.

He lighted a cigarette and waited. There was a fog rolling up from the river, and it softened the garish neon-framed entrance to the diner. If the fog got worse, he decided, he'd move the car closer so he'd be sure not to miss Laurie when she came out.

He saw her then, as she crossed the sidewalk to a Buick sedan parked at the curb. The light from the diner glistened on trim nyloned legs and made a golden nimbus around her long blonde hair, and then she was in the car and the car was drifting away from the curb.

The Buick turned right at the first intersection, in the opposite direction from the rooming house where Laurie lived. Chris stayed well back, but once, at a red light, he came close enough to make out the small red triangle above the Buick's license plate that showed it was a rented car.

They were near the river now, and the fog was thicker. With the heavy fog, Chris knew, there was little chance that the couple in the Buick would discover they were being followed.

The Buick turned onto the highway alongside the river and picked up speed. Ten miles further on, the big car slowed, and suddenly Chris knews its destination. There was an abandoned side road a quarter of a mile from here, one that Laurie had pointed out to him the second or third time he'd taken her out riding. The side road led past a rock quarry to an abandoned reservoir, looped around the reservoir and doubled back on itself. The place where the side road joined the highway was almost hidden by weeds and low-hanging tree branches, and Chris had never known it existed until Laurie pointed it out to him.

It had been their own private lover's lane — for a while. He'd tried not to think of how many others she might have shown it to.

The Buick came to almost a complete stop, then nosed through the weeds and branches and started up the side road.

Chris pulled off the highway to wait until it was safe to follow. He lighted another cigarette and leaned back against the seat, looking at nothing. He was still filled with a sense of wonder at his complete lack of emotion. Other than pity for his father, he'd felt absolutely nothing. And still, he reasoned, the whole situation was very simple. A guy met a girl, and something happened. You knew the girl was no good for you, and yet that made no difference at all. She made the world go round for you, and for the first time in your life you knew what it was to love someone. You'd wanted her body at first, sure — but all at once it was more than that. You couldn't describe how you felt any more than you could understand it, but it was there and it was all that mattered. As long as you had the girl, you were king, and the moment you lost her you knew you didn't care whether you lived or died.

The only thing you knew — really knew — was that you were going to kill the man who'd taken her away from you. That was all you had to hang on to — the certain knowledge that you were going to make him pay for what he'd done to you.

For one brief moment he thought, Am I crazy? Am I really crazy? And then he straightened, tossed the cigarette out the window and released the hand brake.

He followed the winding road until he was near the reservoir.

They'd be parked near here, he knew; there was no other place to go. He was halfway around the reservoir before he spotted the Buick. He cut off his lights and stopped the car, squinting through the fog toward the other car. There was no reason for Laurie and the guy to be alarmed, he knew; they'd think it was just another couple up to the same thing they were.

He heard a door slam. They were leaving the Buick on the driver's side, the side away from him. For just a moment he caught sight of Laurie's blonde head and heard the silver murmur of her laughter as she passed between the front of the Buick and a clump of high bushes, and then he realized the man had already left the car and was there in the bushes waiting for her. At first, he'd thought the man's body was just another shadow.

He knew that particular clump of bushes as well as he knew the interior of his father's car. There was deep, thick grass there, almost completely surrounded by a heavy screen of bushes. A perfect place for the thing Laurie liked best.

He thought of the night he had first found out he was losing her. She'd made him take her straight home from the diner. A splitting headache, she'd said. He'd taken her home and then driven around the block, suspicious of her even then. Half an hour later a Buick had driven up and Laurie had come down the steps and gotten inside.

And he remembered how, later, Laurie's soft mouth had twisted cruelly as she told him the other man knew more about women than Chris would ever know. A real man, she said, and handsome. . . . How handsome would the guy be with a hunting knife twisting around in his belly? He'd suffer, all right, but not any more than he'd caused Chris to suffer.

He lifted his sport shirt and drew out the knife. It was hard and cold against his palm. He tightened his fingers around the handle till his knuckles ached.

And now he knew why he had followed Laurie and the guy all the way up here, why he hadn't waited near Laurie's house until they came home and then followed the guy alone. He knew with sudden clarity that it wasn't just the guy he was going to kill; he was going to kill Laurie too. It must have been in his mind ever since he turned up the side road, he realized, but it had only now become focused and articulate.

He opened the car door softly and stepped out on the grass. From where he stood, he could have seen directly into the clump of bushes where Laurie and the guy were, except that the fog had obscured his view. It was a good thing, that fog, he thought; he'd be able to get right up on them before they saw him.

Until this moment, he had been able to keep his mind off what would happen to his father after this was over. He fought back the memory of his father sitting on the side of his bed with him, trying in his fumbling, clumsy way to warn him against Laurie.

Then, as he stared at the fog-shrouded opening in the clump of bushes, the fog suddenly lifted and he could see them there. Laurie and the man. They were on the ground, their bodies entwined.

Something twisted in Chris' stomach. A sour, hot fluid welled up into his mouth and he clutched at the car door until the feeling passed.

He couldn't go near them, he knew now. He didn't know why, but he simply could not. He dropped the hunting knife to the ground and slid back into the car. There was a better way to do it; a hell of a lot better way. He caught his lower lip between his teeth, choking back the sobs that seemed as though they would burst his chest. He tasted the salty flow of blood in his mouth and spat it out, and then he started the motor.

The fog had drifted back in front of the opening in the bushes now, but that made no difference; he knew exactly where Laurie and the guy were lying.

He turned the car so that it pointed straight at the bushes and pushed down on the gas pedal.

His eyes were wide open when the car hit the bushes. He heard the single meaty impact and felt the sickening jar as the hurtling car slammed into the naked bodies, and then he was fighting the wheel to keep from turning the car over.

When he was on all four wheels again, he turned and drove back toward the bushes.

His headlights picked out Laurie's white body first. He put on the hand brake and got out to look at her. Her head had been almost completely severed from her body. Blood spilled from the jugular, angling down between the upthrust mounds of her breasts.

He turned away and walked slowly toward the other figure.

The man lay on his side, his face turned away from Chris, one arm twisted beneath him and the other thrown up across his eyes as if to ward off the death that had already come. There was a gaping hole in his side, the rib fragments lining the cavity like broken laths in wet red plaster.

Chris knelt down and jerked the man over on his back. The man's arm fell away from his face, bounced, and lay still.

For a single stunned moment Chris saw the face as it must have appeared to a man-hungry girl like Laurie Jackson. It was the face of a man grown gray at the temples, experienced and maturely handsome — the face of a man who would know about women, who would make Chris, by comparison, seem like a baby. . . .

There was a sudden, blinding pain behind Chris' eyes.

"Dad," he whispered. "My God . . . *Dad!*"

MUGGED AND PRINTED

HENRY KANE, one of the small band of lawyers-turned-writers, states he's even busier at a typewriter than he ever was while engaged in his thriving legal practice. As *The Big Touch* proves, he not only still knows his lawbooks, but deserves the worldwide popularity his tough-cookie private richard, Peter Chambers, has received. Chambers has appeared in all but one of Kane's seven novels, which have been reprinted in almost every country in the world, including the Scandinavian.

BRUNO FISCHER *(Coney Island Incident)* just plain doesn't like interviewers. He dodges and runs from them — and, when finally caught, divulges only the merest smattering of information. We've been able to discover, though, that he's the author of seventeen mystery novels (two under a pseudonym he refuses to identify), is an incorrigible Giant fan, along with his wife and children, and resides during the winter months at Croton-on-Hudson, New York. His wife, Ruth, writes confession stories.

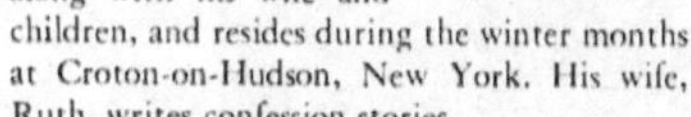

EVAN HUNTER (*The Right Hand of Garth*), who's become an old friend to *Manhunt* readers through his Matt Cordell yarns, is one of the more recent arrivals in the mystery field — and one of the most successful. His recent Popular Library novel, *Don't Crowd Me*, is a booming bestseller, and his stories have appeared in virtually every magazine on the stands, since he also writes science-fiction, Westerns, general fiction, and humor. Mystery and crime, however, remain his first loves.

CRAIG RICE has recently moved to Santa Monica, where she's hard at work on a new movie venture — a picture based on her novel, *Innocent Bystander*, which she's writing for the screen and directing — and in which her daughter will star. Also in the works is a Graphic Books reprint of her best-selling *45 Murderers*, now on the stands. In spite of this loaded schedule, though, Miss Rice hasn't forgotten the wild and wacky John J. Malone. As proof, see the latest Malone yarn, *The Bells Are Ringing*.

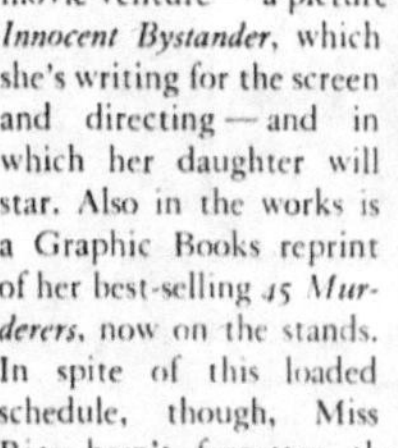

FLETCHER FLORA's been variously compared to James M. Cain and J. D. Salinger — two very different people. All we can say in settlement is that the guy is terrific — and we think you'll agree when you read *A Long Way to KC*. • RICHARD MARSTEN is a victim of wanderlust, having travelled all over the United States. He keeps coming back to New York, however, and to the New York Police Department archives, for his fine documentaries. • CHARLES BECKMAN, JR. is an expert on Texas history who divides his time between Westerns and crime yarns such as the fine *Killing on Seventh Street*. Both fields bear fruit for him, because of his remarkably accurate portrayal of character and scene. • JONATHAN CRAIG, "ex- practically everything," claims his *Kid Stuff* is realistic because, "I'm an ex-teenager myself."

CAPTAIN FUTURE
WIZARD OF SCIENCE
COMET
FICTION AND FACT OF THE PRIZE-RING
FIGHT STORIES
THE BLACK UHLAN
HEADQUARTERS DETECTIVE
MURDER TREADMILL
G-MAN JUGGERNAUT
MASKED RIDER WESTERN
Devil's RANGE
BORROWED HOSSES
FIGHTING ACES OF WAR SKIES
WINGS
10 STORY WESTERN MAGAZINE
POWDERSMOKE PUPPET
SATAN SPAWNS A WOGLIE WAR
ADVENTURE NOVELS
Thrilling Stories of the Sky Trails
Air STORIES
THE NIGHT HAWK
FIGHTING DAREDEVILS OF TODAY'S WAR
AIR WAR
MASK OF GLORY
THE ALL-STORY
WARLORD of MARS
ARMY Romances
BASKETBALL STORIES
GAWKY GUARD
Battle Stories
O'LEARY IN ACTION IN ETHIOPIA
All Star Issue of Favorite War Authors
BLACK BOOK DETECTIVE
GOLDEN FLEECE
HISTORICAL ADVENTURE
ROMAN HOLIDAY by TALBOT MUNDY
HIGH-SEAS ADVENTURES
THE SEA ROGUE
CAPTAIN HARDY
ADVENTURES of the FIRST AMERICANS
INDIAN Stories
BRIDE of the TOMAHAWK PACK
MY LIFE WITH SITTING BULL
LONE RANGER
10
April
MAGIC CARPET MAGAZINE
PEARLS FROM MACAO
MARVEL SCIENCE STORIES
THE TIME TRAP
NEW DETECTIVE
NO BODY BUT YOU
North-West ROMANCES
SATAN'S TIMBER CLAIM
GIRL of the WHITE WATER TRAIL
Oriental Stories
PHANTOM DETECTIVE
The Death's DIAMONDS
PLANET STORIES
QUEEN OF THE MARTIAN CATACOMBS
POPULAR DETECTIVE
DEATH IN A COTTAGE
MURDER INSURANCE
PRIVATE DETECTIVE
NOV 15¢
LOVE STORIES OF THE REAL WEST
RANCH ROMANCES
Maid of the Valley
STORIES OF WESTERN AVENGERS IN ACTION
RANGE RIDERS
SIX-GUN VALLEY
Vice Squad DETECTIVE
SECRET of the HOUSE of HORROR
TOP-NOTCH STORIES ... TOP-NOTCH WRITERS
UNDERWORLD DETECTIVE
FIVE FATAL MINUTES
KILLER'S BAIT
THRILLING WONDER STORIES
THE FEDERALS IN ACTION
G-MEN
GOVERNMENT GUNS
THE BLUE LOTUS
GIVE 'EM HELL
SCIENCE FICTION
PLANET OF THE KNOB HEADS
SPICY-ADVENTURE STORIES
HELL'S RIVER

www.ingramcontent.com/pod-product-compliance
Lightning Source LLC
LaVergne TN
LVHW090959080826
845145LV00003B/1055